CHRIS COPPEL

CRANTHORPE
MILLNER
PUBLISHERS

Table of Contents

LIVING WATER

Chapter 1

Aaron Davies lounged on the back of his 280-foot yacht, *Sea No Evil*. On either side of him were his latest pair of willing girls who hoped that a little of his wealth would rub off on them at the same time as his other bodily fluids. Even at seventy-six years old, he still had the sexual appetite of a teenager. The problem was that despite his cravings, his ability to fully partake of such pleasures was becoming more and more unsatisfactory for all involved. Even with the latest blue pill and synthetic club drugs, Aaron couldn't hide the fact that he was an old man with old-man plumbing and circuitry.

Aaron had been wealthy before 2020 but had made billions more shorting just about any industry he could think of on the first day that Covid had become news. Cruise lines, airlines, hotel and restaurant chains—you name it. His latest few billions had been made guessing which industries would suffer the most at any given time during the crisis. He was by no means the only person to have capitalised on the pandemic, however he seemed to know exactly when each country would next be imposing a lockdown, and just as importantly, when each one would be lifted.

Aaron had sat like a predatory vulture watching Covid numbers rise and fall. By shorting company stocks days before a surge and lockdown, he netted a fortune. When he rebought the stock days prior to restrictions being lifted, he made another windfall.

Wall Street was calling him some sort of devilish parasite feeding off the world's suffering. He didn't agree at all. Aaron felt that he was simply preying on the stupidity of the global population that permitted the pandemic to continue long after it should have been eradicated.

If people hadn't turned the virus into a political ideology over free will, Aaron would not have made the fortune he did. He'd already been one of the more unsavoury adopters of arbitrage: buy a struggling company, rip it apart for its few profitable sections then bury what remained. The result was high profits and massive unemployment.

His hundred-million-dollar portfolio ended up being valued at close to three billion by the end of 2021. The yacht he was lying on was the result of the shorting then repurchasing of large share blocks of Lufthansa and JAL immediately before and at the end of various lockdown periods.

"I'm bored," one of the girls said as she rolled onto her back. "Can't we do something fun?"

Her name was Cindy and she was a member of the cabin crew on Aaron's Gulfstream. She was blonde, twenty-eight and looked like a young Meg Ryan. After providing him with some 'exceptionally good' service on a couple of long-haul flights, he'd rewarded her with a week on his yacht. The other one was Kelly. She was from Virginia and worked in the offices of Hapshire and Kent, the Manhattan legal firm he kept on retainer. She was on the boat as something of a

2

thank you from Giles Hapshire.

Aaron was not the least bit ashamed about accepting the attentions of beautiful young women. Whether it was as payback or just gold-digging he didn't care. At two hundred and eighty pounds, Aaron knew that he was hardly going to end up on the cover of GQ, so if the only way he was going to get a constant supply of hot and cold running women was through his wealth and influence, who was he to argue?

"Maybe we could go ashore for breakfast?" Cindy suggested.

Aaron was about to reply when Martin Wilder, his personal assistant, stepped over to him and whispered in his ear.

"Holy shit," Aaron replied conspiratorially before looking at the two girls and telling them to go play somewhere else. Once they were out of earshot, he said, "What did the text say?"

"It said that the encrypted images have been downloaded direct from the satellite to your personal hard drive. I would have checked them out, but I don't have clearance."

"Nobody does. That's why it's called restrictive."

Aaron swung his girth into a sitting position then after a couple of tries, got to his feet.

"Come down with me. You might as well see what we've got."

They both walked to the yacht's central elevator and rode it down two decks to Aaron's private office, the one that only a small handful of people had ever been given the right to enter.

Aaron held his face close to a retinal scanner and moments later, the steel door slid open.

Martin knew to turn away when Aaron logged into his private network. Aaron first read the auto text confirming the image transmission; the same one that Martin had been copied on.

"This could really be it," Aaron said excitedly as he entered the key to enable the download.

"Looks like it," Martin agreed. "Having your satellite scan the whole grid seems to have paid off. There's no other way we would have found the right mesa in hundreds of square miles of canyons."

"I just hope it isn't just another undiscovered lake?" Aaron said as the first images began to appear on his sixty-inch monitor.

Martin nervously shook back a wave of blond hair that had just fallen forward covering his right eye. He hoped this would be the breakthrough Aaron had been waiting for. Otherwise, he was going to have to deal with another of his boss' violent outbursts. The last one had put Martin in the hospital with a dislocated shoulder.

As the data buffered and the image resolution increased, they could make out hundreds of slot canyons that looked, from that height, to resemble dark veins against the mars-like red hills.

Aaron scrolled through the images and after the initial overview shots, he zoomed in closer on one particular area. At first it was hard to see the blue dot amidst the rough terrain, but as the zoom increased the dot became a blue oval then finally, a small blue lake in the centre of a mesa.

Aaron was stunned; he'd been hearing about the place for over ten years, and until he'd managed to obtain a video actually showing the sacred rites, no amount of investigations or greasing of palms had opened even one mouth. The only prior indication that something interesting was tucked away within Southern Utah's massive maze of unexplored slot canyons was in an early Mormon journal, written by one of Brigham Young's older disciples.

It was only a few paragraphs, but the words left no doubt about what they had discovered.

Within the red valleys where the raging torrents originated, lies the spring. Atop a smaller mesa, and sheltered by high cliffs and soaring spruce, the tranquil water lies. After proving my spirit's worthiness, I was led many miles through tortuously narrow gullies until footfalls became evident in the canyon wall. Once atop the cliff, the waters shone clear and tranquil. The natives that had accompanied me walked me slowly to the shore then gestured for me to enter the water.

It was cold beyond anything I'd ever felt. My skin felt as if pricked by a million needles. The natives gestured for me to lower myself until I was completely submerged. Trusting their tradition, I did as they requested. Before I knew what was happening, a force far stronger than myself took hold of my body and dragged me deeper into the lake.

I could not breathe, and finally, with ebbing strength and lungs afire, I drew in the freezing waters. I remember seeing white lights shimmer all about my body, then within what seemed to be mere seconds, everything faded to black.

I awoke sometime later on the bank of the pool. I was coughing up water and having to gasp to obtain even the slightest breath. The natives that had escorted us to the spot were nowhere to be seen. Neither were my own followers. I was completely alone, cold and, if I'm honest, scared.

Beside me were some plain clothes that I assumed were for me to don considering that I was naked when I entered the water and remained thus. I am not a man who suffers from an excess of vanity and rarely look upon my own body, however, something made me glance down at myself.

The excess weight I had gathered during my seventy-eight years had seemingly melted away. My skin looked unmarked and youthful. I stepped towards the still waters and stared down at my own shimmering reflection.

I was no longer aged. I no longer held the wear that time places on a person's visage. Instead, the face that stared back at me was that of a young man in his late teens. I recognised my younger self from memories many years past.

The water had done what the natives had promised.

They had given me back my youth.

Aaron looked at the images that had been shot from over ten thousand miles above the earth. He could clearly see the lake which he half-expected. What he hadn't imagined being a possibility was seeing a line of Native Americans in full tribal regalia, surrounding the blue water.

Aaron scrolled further but the image quality deteriorated then became blocky and digitized.

"That must be all they could capture," Martin suggested. "Now that we know where it is, we could run another series of..."

"No," Aaron barked. "Nobody must know what we've found. Call Harry on the sat phone and tell him to meet us at St. George airport. Tell him we'll give him an ETA once we're wheels up."

Chapter 2

The Citation jet got them from Cabo St Lucas to St. George, Utah in just under five hours. Harry was waiting in the executive terminal as instructed. Dressed in chino shorts, an old generic T-shirt and hiking boots, nobody would have imagined that he was one of the most lauded geologists in the world.

After a brief conversation on the tarmac, a private helicopter flew them over the town of Kanab, before heading due east for another fifty miles.

Beneath them, the startling red rock landscape looked like a maze designed by a drunk. Slot canyons appeared then vanished only to reform a few hundred feet later. Trying to understand the erosional footprint that had required millions of years to create was like trying to find logic in a bucket full of sand.

Finally, the pilot slowed the Bell 525 and brought it to a hover a thousand feet above one particular mesa formation. As Aaron, Harry and Martin looked down, a cloud above them slid aside allowing the sun to offer the men a clear view of the fabled pool of water.

"Take us down," Aaron instructed.

"There's nowhere to land. Plus, this is as low as we are permitted to go."

"Why?"

"This land belongs to the Shoshone Tribe. The FAA has some very strict regulations regarding what we can and can't do on their land."

"I don't give a shit," Aaron announced. "For what I'm paying you, you should be able to touch down anywhere I damn well please."

"Sorry, sir," the pilot replied. "You're not paying me enough to lose my licence. Besides, that area around the lake is nothing but soft sandstone and loose dirt. We'd likely as not either clog the air intakes or topple over as the ground subsided. Either way, you're going to have to get a permit and find another way to reach the mesa."

"How do we do that?" Martin asked as Aaron sulked, staring down at the clear blue water.

"I'll sort this out," Harry interrupted. "I think we should start with the BLM and see what they suggest."

"What the fuck is the BLM?" Aaron snapped.

"Bureau of Land Management," Harry replied. "The nearest county office is back in Kanab. Why don't we go back there?"

"This was supposed to be easy," Aaron said, glaring at Martin as if the whole thing was his doing.

Once they landed at Kanab's small, single-strip airfield, Aaron looked around for the car that Harry had just rented online but couldn't see it. He walked to the tiny airport office and found that it was locked. Aaron knew there had to be someone around as there was a mud-coated Jeep parked right next to the office.

"Where the hell is the car?" Aaron barked.

Harry opened a text he had just received from a company called Red Rock Excursions. Below the instructions on how to find the key, there was a photo of the vehicle. It was an older model, red Jeep with a dented right-front fender and a broken left-side taillight.

Harry smiled as he approached the parked jeep and after scraping off a layer of mud, found the dented red fender.

"I think this is it," he announced.

"I'm not getting in that piece of shit," Aaron stated.

Harry gestured to the empty, wind-swept airfield.

"I don't think we have much of a choice."

"I don't suppose it has GPS?" Aaron asked.

Harry looked inside. "I don't think it even has a radio," he observed.

"We can just use my iPhone," Martin suggested.

"Are you getting a signal?" Aaron asked.

Martin checked, blinked twice, then looked helplessly back at his boss.

"I didn't think so. Let's just head towards town and see if we can find this BLM place. If not, we should at least be able to find someone who can tell us where it is."

It took a couple of tries for Martin to get the old jeep to turn over, then, when it did, it sounded more like a clogged garbage disposal than a maintained combustion engine.

They turned left onto highway 89A and saw what appeared to be the town only a few miles ahead. The first sign of civilization was a large diesel repair yard off to the left. Judging from the number of rusting hulks in the forecourt, their ability to keep the rigs running was spotty at best.

A few hundred yards further on they passed a sprawling self-storage business followed by a small housing estate on a treeless street named Plum Lane.

Two blocks later they saw a modern, stylishly designed building. The discreet signage read: Kane County, Bureau of Land Management.

"This looks promising," Martin offered.

Aaron didn't share his assistant's optimism and just growled.

Martin pulled up at the main entrance and the three dismounted the Jeep.

Martin went to open the door for Aaron, but it didn't budge. They peered inside through smoked glass windows and couldn't see any sign of life.

"It says here," Martin read from a small, laminated notice taped to the inside of the door, "they don't open on Tuesdays until two-thirty."

"It's only one o'clock," Aaron snarled. "What the hell are we supposed to do until then?"

"I don't know about you two, but I could use something to eat," Harry opined.

"They got any restaurants in this dump?" Aaron asked.

"I would imagine they do. This place is becoming quite a destination."

"Why? We're in the middle of nowhere," Aaron observed.

"I think that may just be the point. It's close to Zion, Bryce and the Grand Canyon. I've heard they're starting to offer glamping vacations."

Aaron stared at Harry as if he was talking complete

gibberish.

"Let's just drive through town and see what they've got," Harry suggested.

The three piled back into the Jeep and headed towards the centre of Kanab. After a brief search, they settled on an unremarkable-looking Mexican restaurant. It was the only one with a parking lot full of cars which had to mean something.

"I'll have a double margarita," Aaron ordered the moment they were seated.

The waitress looked confused.

"Straight tequila if that's all you got," Aaron suggested.

"I'm sorry sir, we have beer, but that's all the alcohol we are licenced for."

Aaron looked at Harry as if the geologist would have some sort of explanation.

Thankfully, he did.

"We're in Southern Utah. Not many places are going to serve hard liquor. You're lucky they even have beer."

Aaron harrumphed and ordered a Corona.

The food was fresh and surprisingly tasty. Aaron, turning on what he believed was his charm, mentioned to the waitress that he had just flown in from his yacht in Cabo and that he'd never had a better burrito even in the popular seaside resort.

She gave him another confused look then retreated back to the kitchen.

With a few minutes to kill before the BLM was scheduled to open, Harry drove through the town to get a better feel for the place.

It was hard to pin down exactly what the planners had been going for. Quaint motels and shops were surrounded by dozens of service stations. Restored Victorian homes sat alongside single-wide trailers that looked ready to topple over.

At the very back of the town, tucked away in its own little valley, was a modern housing development. It looked as if it once could have once had some charm, however the developer had at some point decided to keep building right up against the hills, just below a couple of sizeable slot canyons. Instead of looking like a quiet, high desert neighborhood, it reminded Harry of the San Fernando Valley, just north of Los Angeles; a place where every piece of charm had been paved over and sold as quarter acre lots.

Harry looked to the very back of the development and shook his head.

"Not your style?" Aaron asked.

"It's not that. These idiots have built the homes right up against a pair of slot canyons."

"What's wrong with that?" Martin asked.

"Next big flooding rain; one of the ones that fills those back canyons; the water's going to come out of there like a tidal wave. Probably take half of these homes with it."

Aaron looked at the small lots with their near-identical floorplans and shrugged.

"No great loss."

Chapter 3

They made it back to the BLM offices at two-thirty exactly.
The door was still locked. It wasn't until a few minutes before
three when a well-used Ford F-250 pickup pulled into the lot
and a man got out.

"You folks waiting for me?" he asked.

Harry sensed that Aaron was about to explode at the guy
and replied before he could get up a good head of steam.

"No worries," Harry replied amiably. "Gave us a chance
to snoop around your beautiful town."

"She's not bad is she," the man said as he unlocked the
door. "Usually don't take appointments on a Tuesday, but
since you're here, and I'm here, be kind of
counterproductive not to, don't you reckon?"

Again, Harry spoke before Aaron could get a word in.

"That's mighty kind of you. I'm Harry Granger and this
here's..."

"Harry Granger?' The man said, surprised. "*The Earth
Beneath our Feet,* Harry Granger?"

"One and the same," Harry replied with every
appearance of sincere modesty.

"I make every employee and volunteer read your book
before they even get started working for the BLM."

"Myself and my publishers thank you," Harry replied with

a wink and a nod of gratitude.

"The name's Gary Kinkaid." Gary held out a hand and Harry shook it enthusiastically. "I gotta tell you, this is a real honour for me. Your book gives people more reason to give pause and appreciate what's under our feet than any book, TV show or classroom lecture that I have ever heard of."

"That's very kind of you, Gary. I'd like you to meet Aaron Davies and Martin Wilder. They're out here to get a little bit of local knowledge about the slot canyons and such."

Gary shook their hands with new-found enthusiasm.

"Well, if there's any information that I have, I'd be mighty proud to share it. Let's go back into our little conference room and have ourselves a chat."

Once settled around the table, Harry produced a blow-up of a regional survey map. The lake in question had been circled in red.

"We would like permission to visit this area, ideally by helicopter."

Gary looked at the map, then at the three men sitting around the table.

"I'm sorry, but we don't have jurisdiction over that area. In addition, visiting it is completely impossible. It's a holy site belonging to the Shoshone Tribe. I've known many people try to get approval to trek up there, and all have been refused. Access to the Sacred Mesas is by invitation only."

"So how do we get one of those invitations?" Aaron asked.

"By having been someone who has shown great kindness to the Shoshone people or has somehow benefitted the Native American culture."

"Sounds to me like they just want a nice fat donation," Aaron surmised.

"I think you'll find they require way more than that."

"What's more important than having enough money to buy themselves anything they'll ever need?"

"Goodness of soul," Gary replied.

Aaron looked about to argue the point when Harry spoke first.

"Who specifically does the inviting?"

"The Tribal Council."

"And how do we get an appointment to meet with them?"

"You don't. They meet at unscheduled places and times. The only thing I can suggest is that you contact their lawyer. Hightower might be able to explain things better than I'm doing."

"Where do we find this guy?" Aaron asked trying to mask his growing frustration.

"*She* has an office in Cedar City. I'll write down her details."

"Will she be able to get us up to the … what did you call it? The Sacred Mesas?"

"I doubt it, but she will at least be able to give you more detail about the site and the restrictions."

"Let me ask you this in another way." Aaron leaned forward on the laminated table. "We did our best to come here and ask permission, but what if we just fly there without anyone's approval. I mean, it's in the middle of nowhere. Say we find a place to land, hike a little, then check out the area and see what all the fuss is about. Is anyone really gonna mind?"

"I can't answer that question," Gary stated bluntly.

"Why the fuck not? I'm guessing that hundreds of people have hiked up there before."

"You'd be right, yes."

"Exactly. So what do they say happened?"

"They don't say anything."

"Why not?"

"Because none of them have ever been seen again."

Chapter 4

When they reached the waiting helicopter, Harry called the number Gary had given them. Suzie Hightower answered the phone herself.

"I was expecting your call," she said.

"I guess Gary called to warn you," Harry replied.

"No. I got a call minutes after you initially flew over the mesa."

"Then you know why we want to speak with you."

"I can guess."

"We're in Kanab at the moment but could be in Cedar City in just over an hour."

Suzie laughed. "You're presuming that I will make time for you."

"What have you got to lose? We'll pay your regular rate plus a donation that you can spread among the tribespeople."

"How big a donation?" she asked.

"A thousand dollars. That's just for the meeting. If this goes well, I can guarantee substantially more."

"I'll tell you what, make the donation for ten thousand dollars and I'll open up my calendar."

"Ten thousand?" Harry stared at Aaron, who shrugged then nodded. "Ok, we can do that."

"My office is at 250 South Main Street. I'll expect you at five o'clock."

The call disconnected.

They arrived at her office at four thirty and were led to a simple but tastefully decorated waiting room.

Suzie kept them sitting there until close to six.

"Sorry to have kept you waiting," she said as she walked into the room. "We've been having a problem with an animal charity in Kanab that continually encroaches on our tribal lands."

The three men could only stare up at her.

Suzie was striking. Just over six feet, she had waist-length black hair tied back with a turquoise clip, broad shoulders and a narrow waist. She was wearing jeans, snakeskin boots and a blue T-shirt that perfectly matched her eyes.

"If I understand you correctly, you wish to visit our sacred pool out beyond Smokey Hollow."

"That's right," Harry replied. "Obviously, we understand the importance of the area and want to make sure we have permission."

"Firstly, it's not my land. It is owned by my people as a whole. Secondly, while I appreciate your statement about wanting permission before visiting the site, perhaps you could explain why you spent so much time in your helicopter looking for a suitable landing area."

"We were just checking it out," Aaron replied. "We wanted to make sure we had the right place."

"The right place for what?"

Before Aaron could answer and most likely say the wrong thing, Harry jumped in.

"We've heard tell of the waters within the pool and were curious as to the validity of the stories. These days, you can't believe ninety percent of what you hear."

"And what is it exactly that you have heard that would bring you all the way out here? Especially you, Mr Davies. Flying all the way from Cabo San Lucas is quite a trip."

Aaron's face grew crimson. "Now see here, missy, you know exactly what the rumours are about the pool. People say it's filled with water that can stop aging and sometimes even turn back the clock altogether."

"And you believe this because of a few stories you've picked up … I assume online?"

Aaron grinned. "No. I believe it because of this."

He laid his oversized iPhone on the table. On the screen was an image of sparkling blue water surrounded by harsh red cliffs. He pressed the play icon, and the image came to life. An elderly tribesman, naked as the day he was born, was being helped to the water's edge. The man looked ancient and frail.

Another tribesman, this one dressed in the ceremonial garb of a shaman, spoke a few unintelligible words to which the elderly man answered.

The shaman nodded then stepped closer to the man. He produced a pouch from which he removed a small, dark blue flower, the like of which Aaron and his team had never seen before.

The old man opened his mouth, and the shaman placed the bud on his tongue.

Two young men took their place on either side of the elderly man and led him slowly into the water. They moved cautiously as the water deepened. Soon they were at waist height. The young men stepped away and walked back on shore.

The man, now alone in the pool, looked up once towards the heavens, then let himself fall backwards into the water, submerging himself completely.

The water stilled and for almost sixty seconds nothing happened until a ripple appeared on the surface. Suddenly the water roiled and from the centre of the disturbance, a young, naked man rose up, his arms raised to the sky as he began to walk back to the shore.

The old man appeared to have lost eighty years.

"Does that look like a rumour?" Aaron asked.

"I can show you a video of a dinosaur destroying San Diego," Suzie stated. "You mustn't believe everything you see on YouTube."

"I didn't see that on YouTube," he replied with a smirk plastered on his face. "This was shot by an investigator of mine using a drone. It was far enough away for there to have been no noise, but you have to admit, the video quality is spectacular."

Suzie studied him. "When was this shot?"

Aaron glared at her.

"Over a year ago," Martin replied.

"Yet you have waited this long to venture out here? Surely your investigator must have given you all the details of the location back then?"

"Actually, he didn't," Aaron said. "Once he'd sent us the video, he demanded double the agreed amount to reveal the location."

"Why didn't you pay him? You clearly have the means."

"We were going to but he disappeared," Martin answered. "No one has seen or heard from him since that day."

"That's the problem with those slot canyons," Suzie commented. "One can so easily get turned around and never find a way out."

"Are you going to help us or not?" Aaron snapped.

"What exactly do you want?" she asked, her voice emotionless.

"I want to be allowed up there to that pool and be given the same ceremony. I want to be young again."

"Impossible. What you saw is one of the most secretive rites of my people. It is only rarely performed and never to an outsider such as yourself."

"Then it just may be time to change that policy."

"The tribal council will not permit you to take part in the ceremony," Suzie stated.

"What if I made it worth their while," Aaron suggested. "I'm a wealthy man. I'm sure that your tribal leaders could do some wonderful things with the right amount of money."

"And what do you feel is the right amount of money?"

"I was thinking around a million."

Suzie laughed.

"What's so funny?" Aaron barked; he was clearly not used to being laughed at.

"To be blunt … you," Suzie replied. "You are worth in excess of three billion dollars, yet to be given the chance to basically live your entire life for a second time, you are only willing to pay what you would earn in interest alone in one day. That tells me that either you don't value yourself very highly, which I doubt, or that you take us for complete fools."

"There is of course a third option," Aaron said as he leaned back in his chair.

"And that is?"

"You accept my generous offer, and I won't release the video. That's the funny thing about the internet, all I have to do is to place it on ... I don't know, let's start with Instagram. My guess is that it will go viral within twenty-four hours and by the end of the first seven days will have received at least a billion views. If I tag the video with the location, there will be so many incursions on your land that nothing and nobody will be able to stop every nut job with the means to try out the magic pool."

"What's to stop you doing that anyway even if we let you up there?"

"Selfishness," Aaron replied. "In case you haven't read about me, I don't really give a shit about anyone else. I would prefer to keep the video and location hidden from the rest of the world. That way, if every ten years or so I want to drop by for another dip, I can."

Suzie took a moment to further study Aaron.

"I will have to first speak with the tribal council," she said.

"Speak with whoever you need to." Aaron smiled.

"Before I do that, I think it's wise for me to briefly tell you the history of the waters, at least as it has been passed down."

"Sure, why not. I can't wait to hear a story about a pool of water."

"I suggest you listen closely and understand what I am

going to tell you."

Aaron rolled his eyes and jabbed Harry in the ribs with his elbow. "This oughta be good."

Chapter 5

"When white men moved west and settled wherever they saw fit, they initially chose arable land abutting areas where Native American tribes had already settled. For a while the white man was content to share the plains between what is now called Kanab and what has become Lake Powell. As their families grew in size, so did their need for more farmland.

"After numerous skirmishes with the Shoshone people where the young males were targeted so that the tribes could never retaliate, the Shoshone wolf god, Issa, appeared one night and led the people to a series of hidden canyons. As they watched, Issa took his wolf form and climbed to the top of a hidden mesa. He howled into the night for hours until, without warning, bolts of lightning shot down from the heavens and created a large depression on the top of the mesa. Within moments, the skies unleashed a torrent of rain that soon filled the hole.

"Issa returned to human form and led all the elderly tribesmen up to the clear waters. Growing by the side of the pool were flowers that no one had ever seen before. Issa explained that each tribesman had to eat one bud then walk into the water and fully immerse themselves.

"Fully trusting their god, each tribesman did as instructed and after rising back up from the water, had miraculously change back into their younger selves. Issa told them that with their young bodies and the older histories still in their minds, they would be able to stop any further encroachments by the farmers and lead the tribespeople into a new period of peaceful existence.

"When asked by the tribespeople why the white men wouldn't use the waters for the same purpose, Issa replied that the powers only existed for the good of the Shoshone and that nobody else would ever benefit from the living water."

Harry, Martin and Aaron stared at Suzie for a long time.

"Wow," Aaron finally said, "that was some story all right. I know you folks love to come up with supernatural reasons for just about everything, but you know what? I created a pool on my property in Connecticut and didn't need a wolf man or any god to help me out. We just dug a hole in March and were swimming in it by Memorial Day."

"I only wanted you to be aware of the legend of the waters before things went any further," Suzie replied calmly.

"Noted," Aaron said. "What's the next step?"

"I will speak to the council and explain the situation."

"Then what?"

"If they agree to you visiting the pool -"

"Which they will," Aaron interrupted.

"You will need to make arrangement to reach the mesa," Suzie continued. "It's not easily accessible."

"I'll take care of that part," Harry said. "I'm sure that ATVs will get us there."

"Good," Aaron said nodding.

As they walked out of the office building, Martin asked,

"Do you want me to arrange hotel rooms here or in Kanab?"

"Do I look like I'm going to stay in a hotel that looks like it's straight out of *Psycho*? I have a much better idea of where to stay."

Aaron called the waiting pilot and asked him to get clearance to a place he knew just outside of Big Water on route 89 on the way to Page, Arizona.

The pilot flew the group over Zion National Park then the famed Vermilion Cliffs before crossing 89. After that, the desert lost all contrast and became a flat eternity of sun-bleached dirt.

After fifteen minutes of bouncing thermals, they circled above the Skylight Arch trailhead then descended between towering rock outcroppings before setting down on an immaculate helipad in the middle of nowhere.

Uniformed staff appeared, seemingly out of thin air, and helped the three alight from the chopper and took what little baggage they had. They climbed onto a custom 6-seater golf cart and within minutes were whisked into the hotel lobby that looked to have been carved out of solid rock.

After setting into their individual suites, all comped by Aaron, they met in the hotel bar where Aaron ordered himself a double cognac. Harry couldn't help noticing on the menu that a single shot of the amber liquid that his boss had chosen cost more than his first car.

"How long do you think they'll make us wait?" Aaron asked.

"Usually these tribal issues can take years before any agreement is reached, but I think that you lit a pretty good fire under that lawyer woman," Harry replied. "I bet she was on the phone the minute we left."

"Were you serious about never releasing the video?" Martin asked. "I mean, there must be some way of making some serious money if this thing really pans out."

Aaron gulped down five hundred dollars' worth of cognac then held the glass above his head, signalling that he wanted more.

"If that little pool of water does what I hope it does, then I plan to find a way of buying back that piece of land from those Indians, levelling all those fucking canyons that surround the place and build the most expensive fucking spa the world has ever seen."

"What about the tribespeople?" Harry asked, concerned.

"Fuck the tribe. Those congressmen we bought and paid for can finally get off their fat asses and do some work. We'll get that parcel put under eminent domain on some pretext of national security, then after a few months, it will be decided that the land isn't suitable for the government, and they will sell it to me. It'll all be done nice and legal."

"They won't be happy," Harry said, sipping his light beer.

"I'm not in the business of making people happy. I'm in the business of making money!"

"If the video of the ceremony has already been shared, what's to stop it going viral before you can get rights to the land?" Harry asked.

"The video hasn't been shared. Once I received my copy and the investigator vanished, I kept it on a hard drive in the one place where nobody will be able to access it."

"Where's that?" Martin asked.

"You were sunbathing about fifty feet away from it only

a few days ago," Aaron said, smirking.

"It's on Sea No Evil?"

"Safest place I know."

"What about the satellite data?" Harry asked.

"All records of the mapping were erased and only one digital copy remains."

"Let me guess." Harry smiled. "Locked away on the yacht?"

Before Aaron could reply, his phone rang. He saw that the caller was Suzie Hightower.

"That was quick," he remarked as he put his phone on speaker.

"You made a very persuasive case," she replied. "They have agreed to your terms but do have one condition over and above what we discussed."

"Let's hear it."

"They will only grant you access to the waters if you abide by all our traditions – including the fact that we will only permit one person to accompany you."

"*One* person? How the hell are two of us supposed to travel fifty miles back into those canyons? Rent camels?"

"Of course not. You may use whatever means you wish for the first part of the journey then you will be met as you near the Living Water Mesa. At that point, the rest of your colleagues will have to return to the trail head by the highway."

"What if I say no?"

"Then you will not be permitted to take part in the ritual."

"What's to stop me just jumping in the water whenever I want?"

"Nothing, if all you want is a refreshing swim. If, however, your wish is for the years to be taken away from you, then you will have to undertake the tradition ritual."

Aaron thought for a moment. "Okay. I'll agree to that," he said as he shook his head for the benefit of Martin and Harry.

Once he hung up, he knocked back another thousand dollars' worth of booze.

"Are you really going to cross them?" Martin asked.

"Absolutely. I'm not going back in those hills without you guys."

"What if they won't let you reach the mesa?" Harry asked.

"Don't you worry, I'll work something out."

After a night of gluttonous dining and drinking, the three met outside the elite spa hotel at six the following morning. A black Range Rover and a driver was waiting for them. Also parked in front of the hotel were two off-road flatbeds, each carrying four ATVs. In addition, four men, each wearing side arms and matching white T-shirts with their security company logo discretely embroidered on the front, leaned against an unbranded off-road SUV. With its tinted windows, oversized bumpers, winches and even a deep-water snorkel, the thing looked like something out of *Mad Max*.

Standing alone, smoking a thin cheroot, was the leader of the team. He was half the size of the security guys but looked twice as dangerous.

"Glad you could make it, Ben," Aaron called out to him.

Ben slowly lifted the brim of his worn cowboy hat and

gave Aaron a simple nod before lowering it again to shield his eyes from the harsh, rising sun.

"That guy gives me the creeps," Martin said, his voice barely above a whisper. "I don't know why you keep using him."

"Yes, you do. There aren't that many men willing to do the sort of work I need done occasionally. Ben has never once questioned my assignments or failed to carry them out."

Martin looked over at Ben, then involuntarily shivered.

The convoy set out ten minutes later. Ben led the way in his own customised off-road vehicle. The MV850 looked like a cross between and ATV and an old-style military jeep. A gun rack with an assortment of long guns took up the space where the back seats would normally have been.

They drove down to highway 89 then turned left. After a couple of miles, Ben turned right onto an unmarked dirt road. The going was rough, hot and dusty as the vehicles kicked up clouds of loose dirt.

After almost an hour, they entered a tight gully. In places the towering red rock walls almost touched the flatbeds. Fifteen minutes later they reached a widening of the canyon.

"Time to transfer to the ATVs," Ben's voice crackled out of the numerous walkie-talkies.

Once they had parked and started unloading the off-road vehicles, Aaron approached Ben.

"You're certain we can reach the mesa with the ATVs?"

"That satellite footage you forwarded to me was like a road map. I know exactly which canyons to follow. That's not saying that we won't run into some obstructions, but these vehicles are pretty good at getting over rough terrain. In the worst case, I have enough explosives in my vehicle to clear a path all the way to Colorado."

Once all equipment and personnel were transferred over, the convoy continued deeper into the maze of ever-narrowing canyons. Most of the red rock walls were so close together that the group had to proceed in single file. What was most disconcerting was that the farther they ventured into the unchartered terrain, the darker and colder it became.

Many of the slot canyons seemed to close overhead as their opposing clifftops almost touched.

Aaron was finding the going harder than the others. His weight, age and lack of fitness made riding the uncomfortable and noisy four wheel off-roader almost unbearable. His legs had gone numb twice and the convoy had had to stop so he could walk around until some sensation returned.

Two hours later they reached an opening in the canyon that Ben had suggested they use as a place to rest, fill their tanks from the strapped-on jerry cans and eat whatever lunch they'd brought with them.

What Ben hadn't been expecting was a welcoming party.

Especially not one as heavily armed as the tribesmen appeared to be.

Chapter 6

The hired security team reacted exactly as they were trained to do and reached for their weapons. None of them had been prepared for dozens of mud-covered figures to emerge from the red walls of the canyon and disarm them before their hands even reached their guns. Ben had his hand on the grip of his 50 calibre Desert Eagle, ready to bring the gun to bear, but as four more tribesmen emerged from the wall only a few inches away from him, he chose to leave the weapon right where it was.

A lone figure emerged from one of the adjoining slot canyons. It took Aaron and the others a moment to recognise Suzie Hightower.

"We will be escorting Mr Davies from this point," she announced as she approached the group.

"The hell you will," Aaron shouted back at her. "These are my personal escorts and as such have every right to accompany me and ensure my safety."

"Your safety is now our responsibility. Besides, none of your vehicles will be of any use from this point on, so unless you plan to walk the next ten miles, I suggest you come with us."

Aaron was about to reply when every vehicle in their convoy went silent. When the group tried to restart their engines, nothing happened.

"The batteries have all been drained," Ben stated as he checked his gauges.

"It's up to you," Suzie said smiling at Aaron. "If you want to visit the living water, you only have one option."

A tribesman appeared out of the same slot canyon leading a large chestnut mare.

"You're not expecting me to get on that thing, are you?" he replied.

"As far as what you chose to do with your future, I have no expectations whatsoever." Suzie shrugged.

Aaron looked to the mud splattered tribesmen then to the horse, then back to Suzie.

"I'll tell you what. We'll forget the security team, but I insist that both my two companions that you met earlier be allowed to accompany me."

"Insist all you want, but in case you haven't yet noticed, you hold no authority out here. You are a guest, be it an unwanted one, and as such will follow our traditions. Every visitor to the mesa is permitted one friend or family member to accompany them. You may choose who that will be."

Aaron, sensing the futility of trying to argue the point looked at Martin then Harry.

"I'll make it easier, boss," Martin said nervously. "Take Harry. This is more his kind of thing than mine."

Aaron turned to Martin. "You don't get to make the decisions. I'll say who I want to go with me."

"I'll pass," Martin replied. "It's all yours, Harry."

"You always were gutless," Aaron said, shaking his head. "You and I are going to have a long talk when we get back to the boat. In fact, why wait? You can go back to the hotel and start making plans for our departure first thing tomorrow. Once you've done that, consider yourself fired."

Aaron then turned to Suzie. "I nominate Harry to come with me."

"Good choice," she replied, trying to keep the sarcasm out of her voice. "Martin, I believe that you will find that the last ATV will now start. You may take that and leave. White marks have been left on the canyon walls to guide you back to where you left the vehicles."

Martin knew he should feel some sort of anger or sadness but felt nothing but relief. Without looking back at Aaron, he walked to the last ATV in line, kicked the starter and just as Suzie had promised, the engine roared to life.

A second horse appeared from the slot canyon. Harry, being used to trekking the terrain on horseback, swung himself onto the saddle.

"There's no way on this earth that I'm going to be able to do that," Aaron stated. "Someone will have to bring me steps or a ladder."

Instead, two tribesmen each grabbed a leg and arm, then with him already in a sitting position, placed Aaron on the second horse.

Suzie tuned to face the remaining men. "We will continue the journey unescorted. You will remain here. If any of you attempt to follow us, there will be repercussions."

Ben glared at her from under the brim of his hat. He was already calculating how long to wait before his team should start following their trail.

Aaron hadn't been on a horse since he was a teenager

and almost immediately remembered why. The saddle was digging into his butt sending waves of pain up his spine. After complaining repeatedly to Suzie, she advised him that he was lucky that they were using the more comfortable western style of saddle rather than the traditional one used by the Shoshone. She also offered him the chance to walk as she was doing, thus eliminating the pain of riding altogether.

Aaron stopped complaining. Walking through the brutal territory would have been impossible for him in his condition. He wondered how much farther they would have to go before his security team caught up with them.

As they continued through the maze of canyons, their numbers diminished as tribesmen broke away and headed off in different directions. Soon, there were only five left. Aaron, the two tribesmen that had hoisted him onto the horse, Suzie and Harry.

"How much farther do we have to go?" Aaron asked in a pained voice.

"Not much farther," Suzie assured him.

Twenty-five minutes later they entered the narrowest slot canyon yet. The top of the walls were so close together that daylight wasn't reaching the trail.

Harry was so fascinated by the geology of his surroundings that he hadn't even noticed the diminishing light. Aaron, on the other hand, was finding it claustrophobic. What made it worse was that the narrow canyon was humid and reeked of sulphur and the ionization that occurs right after a lightning strike.

"Is this smell normal?" Aaron asked.

"No," Harry answered. "I've never encountered anything

like it, not in the high desert anyway."

"Where have you encountered it?"

"Near an active volcano," Harry replied.

Before Aaron could say anything else, they emerged from the canyon into a clearing, roughly the size of a basketball court. The smell of sulphur was even stronger, and he couldn't help noticing that the rock walls appeared to be covered in a florescent, blue moss."

"What the fuck is that shit?" he asked.

Suzie signalled for the group to stop then looked back at Aaron and smiled.

"We're here."

Harry and Aaron were instructed to dismount.

"We have to proceed on foot from now on," Suzie advised.

"You've got to be kidding," Aaron said as he tried to get his left leg over the back of his horse.

"If you prefer, I can have you carried up the to the mesa," she suggested.

Aaron glanced over at the two tribesmen and saw the gleam in their eyes as if already planning how to make the trek even more unpleasant for him.

"I'll walk," Aaron announced as he managed to lower himself to the ground.

Suzie led them to the far end of the clearing then seemed to vanish. It wasn't until Aaron reached the last place they'd seen her that he saw that the rock walls overlapped at that point, giving the appearance of a secret entrance to the next canyon.

When Aaron stepped through the narrow passageway,

he saw that instead of another endless slot canyon, he was faced with a rough-hewn staircase that had been carved out of the canyon wall.

He looked up and saw that it led up to the cliff top.

It wasn't an easy climb. On more than one occasion, Aaron lost his footing and had to be helped by one of the tribesmen. After what seemed like an eternity, they crested the top of the canyon wall.

"Holy shit," Aaron exclaimed.

Less than twenty feet away from him was the pool.

Chapter 7

The water was opaque and the colour of a fine turquoise stone. Aaron couldn't be sure but thought that it might even be emitting a faint glow. The pool was about twenty feet wide and forty feet long. Its banks were made of smooth, red rock that looked to have been polished by time and use.

Standing waiting a few feet from the water's edge were four members of the tribal council. All were wearing their traditional, ancestral attire.

One man approached Aaron, stopping less than a foot away from him.

"Mr Davies, this is Chief Changing Rock. He is the head of the council as well as the tribal shaman. He will guide you through your journey."

"Can we just get on with it?" Aaron felt out of breath and irritable after the long trek.

"No," the chief replied. "First you must understand what it is that you are about to undertake."

"I already know all about it. I saw the video, remember?"

"What you saw was an elderly council member who had served his people for his entire life and wanted the chance to be given more time so that his service could continue."

"Whatever, it doesn't matter to me. What matters is that the guy went into the pool old and came out young."

"The living water is not simply a fountain of youth, Mr Davies. It was sent to us by the gods so that our elderly could be given more time to help the needs of the tribe."

"I am helping the needs of the tribe. I've coughed up some serious money to do this. That should help you people get a few more big screen TVs and fancy cars."

"The living water does indeed bring youth back to the aged, however, it also recognises and judges the inner goodness within each person. It is upon such insight that it knows how far back to take the person."

"The video showed an old guy go back to when he was in his twenties. That will do just fine."

The chief looked long and hard at Aaron.

"We shall proceed," he said finally as he raised his hands to the heavens.

The two tribesmen who had accompanied Aaron up to the mesa approached him and began to undress him.

"Whoa! What the fuck is this?"

"Everyone who enters the living water much do so without any clothing or adornments. That means no clothes, jewellery, watches … nothing."

"You can't expect me to just drop trou in front of you people."

"We can if you want to step into the pool," Suzie said. "If not, we are happy to escort you back to where you left your ATVs."

Aaron glanced at the tribespeople and could see that Suzie was being deadly serious.

"Harry, what do you think?"

Harry shrugged. "This is your fantasy, Aaron. It doesn't

look like it's going to happen unless you get undressed."

"Jesus," Aaron barked. "Can everyone please at least look the other way.

Harry did turn away.

The others did not.

"Fine," Aaron said shaking his head. "You want to see what I got. Here goes."

Aaron rapidly undressed then stood naked as he defiantly glared at the others.

The shaman stepped up to him. "Please open your mouth."

Aaron did as he was told, only because he'd seen that part of the ceremony of the video.

The shaman placed a bright blue flower bud on Aaron's tongue before holding his hands out over the blue water.

"Now we are ready." he announced as he began chanting in a language Aaron had heard on the video and did not understand. Slate grey clouds suddenly appeared overhead and within seconds plunged the mesa into darkness. The only illumination was the glow from the pool.

After about five minutes, the chief signalled to the two tribesmen to help Aaron into the water. They walked him slowly into the pool as Aaron looked down, expecting something to happen.

When he was submerged to waist height, the tribesmen left him standing alone in the azure water.

"Stand where you are," Chief Changing Rock called to him. "This is your last chance to change your mind."

"Ain't going to happen," Aaron called back.

The shaman shook his head and audibly sighed.

"Then keep walking towards the far side of the pool."

Aaron took a step forward expecting something magical to happen.

Nothing did.

He took two more steps by which time the water was almost shoulder height.

"Nothing seems to be happening," he called out a millisecond before he sank beneath the surface.

Harry attempted to run towards the pool but was restrained from getting any closer. All he could do was watch as the surface of the water began to ripple then undulate, sending small waves to the shore.

The faint glow they had perceived when they first saw the water had grown stronger. The centre of the pool glowed brightly as the surface became even more agitated.

"He's not coming out," Harry shouted. "You need to help him."

"Nobody can enter the living water while its energy is active," Suzie advised.

"He's going to die out there."

"That was always a possibility."

After ten more minutes of ever-increasing roiling of the water, Harry realised that Aaron was not coming back.

"We should call somebody," he said to no one in particular.

They ignored him as they moved closer to the waters edge. The illumination within the pool began pulsating. The two tribesmen, somehow innately knowing when the time was right, stepped into the water which almost immediately calmed at the same time as the light dimmed then extinguished entirely.

The two men stood in the centre of the pool until a shape began to emerge from the dark water. The men bent over and gently lifted something into the air.

Because of the darkness, it took Harry a moment to realise what he was seeing. The men were holding a young boy in their hands. He guessed the child was around three or four years old.

The men carried him out of the pool to where the tribal council members were waiting with towels. They accepted the boy and began drying him with as much care as a new mother.

"What just happened?" Harry asked as he stepped over to Suzie.

"His transformation was successful," she said.

"But that's not Aaron," Harry replied.

"Of course, it is. Only it's Aaron when his mind was still pure, and a willingness existed to dedicate his life to helping others."

Before Harry could say anything else. The tribal councillors began walking away from the pool towards the steps.

"Where are they going with him?" Harry asked, while sensing that he didn't want to know the answer.

"They are taking him back to their settlement where he will be raised as one of their own."

"That's impossible. He doesn't belong to them," Harry blurted out.

"Where else could he go? He has no family. No parents to raise him and even you must be able to see the benefits of his being raised to be a caring and giving person rather that what he had become."

"I still don't understand what happened here," Harry whispered.

"The living water reacts to a person's inner goodness when reverting the old to the young. Its energy had to find a time in Aaron's life when goodness was at its strongest. In his case it was when he was still very young. I have to wonder what happened to him as a young boy that changed his moral direction at such a young age."

"I'm not sure, but I think that Aaron's father died when he was around four years old."

"That might partially explain it."

"So, what happens now?" Harry asked.

"This is where we part company," she said with a sad smile.

Before Harry could say anything else, the shaman stepped up to him and whispered something unintelligible into his ear. As Harry turned to face him, Chief Changing Rock blew a silvery powder into Harry's face.

Chapter 8

Harry could hear distant knocking but had no idea where the sound was coming from. As he slowly awakened, he realised that he was still in bed and that the knocking was coming from outside the door.

"Harry. Wake up," Martin called from the hallway.

Harry had no idea why the guy sounded so frantic. They weren't scheduled to leave for the Mesa for another hour.

"I'm coming," he shouted as the knocking continued.

Once he'd put on the hotel's complimentary terrycloth robe, he opened the door and let the other man in.

"What's the matter?" Harry asked. "I was trying to sleep."

"What do you mean, what's the matter?" Martin shouted back. "Where's the convoy and most importantly, where the fuck is Aaron?"

"I don't know what you're talking about. We're not supposed to be leaving for another hour. Why are you panicking?"

"The convoy left yesterday. What's wrong with you?"

"I'm afraid the problem may be with you," Harry replied calmly. "We're scheduled to leave on Thursday morning at sunup."

"Which was yesterday," Martin yelled at him.

"That's not possible," Harry said, shaking his head as he

picked up the TV remote. He turned it on and pressed the CNN tab.

Two things hit him at once. The first was the news item that the station was covering. A helicopter was circling over open ocean as a lower third declared that the yacht belonging to the billionaire, Aaron Davies, had mysteriously sunk off the coast of Mexico. The second shock was the date stamp on the screen. It said that it was Friday, June 29.

"Where's the convoy?" Martin asked, trying to sound in some sort of control of his emotions.

"I don't know," Harry replied. "I have no memory of yesterday at all."

"You don't remember us all driving into the canyons then changing over to ATVs?"

"No, but if you do, then you must know what happened," Harry pointed out.

"I have no idea! The police, the FBI and just about every other law enforcement department have been scouring the area. There's no trace of the original transport vehicles, the ATVs or the security team. They've all just vanished."

"What about the pool? They must be able to find that from the satellite images that Aaron got. Aaron said…"

"That they were on his yacht," Martin finished as he looked over at the TV which was still covering the sinking of the mega yacht.

A newsreader said in a grave voice, "The yacht, *Sea No Evil*, mysteriously sank in an exceptionally deep part of the waters off Cabo St Lucas. The Mexican Navy has stated that they will not attempt any form of salvage operation at a depth of over twelve hundred feet. The cost and the danger to the salvage team make it impossible to even consider."

"All his personal documents were on that stupid boat," Martin sighed.

"So, what happens now?" Harry asked.

"We wait until they find him," Martin said with feigned hope.

*

Within a large cave deep within the unmapped maze of slot canyons in the far south of Utah, the tribal council met for the first time since Aaron's transformation. The ceremony had been simple and brief. The young boy had been formally adopted into the tribe and been given the name, Daina Baa' or boy of the water. In the months that had passed since the billionaire had vanished, the documents that had been found in the hotel safe where he was last seen before the start of his ill-fated expedition into the slot canyon's, were finally recognised to be legitimate and binding.

Almost everyone had heard of Aaron Davies, and all had a pretty good idea of the type of man he was. That's why, when the new codicil to his will left his entire fortune to The Native American Rights Foundation, people were stunned. Social media was overwhelmed with comments from around the world. Apart from the obligatory bigoted voices that cloud so many sites, the overwhelming consensus was shock and delight, that even a man as heartless as Aaron Davies could, even at the end of their life, change course and do the right thing.

LIGHTNING STRIKE

Chapter 1

Marvin Wiseman hated storms. There was no logical reason for such feelings other than some deep-seated belief that there was something innately terrifying and evil about lightning, thunder, wind and rain.

According to the Weather Channel, the storm that had been brewing over the Pacific for a few days finally hit the coastline at around 7:00 pm the previous night. It would reach Marvin's home in Southern Utah within the next few hours, and from what was being reported, it was going to carry one hell of a punch.

As Marvin studied the evening sky, he could see a solid line of dark grey clouds approaching from the west. It almost looked as if a hatch cover was being pulled across the heavens as it blotted out the remaining vestiges of the evening's last light.

Marvin sighed knowing there was nothing much he could do about something as uncontrollable as a severe Pineapple Express. The house was well-built and everything within it was automated and designed to keep him safe. All that was left was to make himself comfortable and ride out the storm.

Having full confidence in his home was not a sentiment that came easily or cheaply. He'd had it built to his own security requirement. The walls and the foundation alone were double the normal thickness of an average home. He'd even had massive girders piled down over fifty feet into the ground as an additional anchor. The windows were blast proof and were actually sunk into the reinforced concrete so that nothing was ever going to shift them.

His 24,000 watts, water-cooled, emergency generator, housed in an indestructible bunker, was less than a month old and could run everything in the house for an indefinite period. With a hotel-size, walk-in freezer and a 500 square foot emergency larder, he had enough food and water to last a year at least.

Though Marvin fit the description of your average survivalist, he'd only recently adopted the mindset. Just over a year earlier, he'd been living three hours north of Los Angeles in a four-bedroom beach house only a few miles from his office within the headquarters of what had been his latest start-up: E-Bridge Inc.

Marvin had formed E-Bridge after creating a universal API (Application Programming Interface) that could open an operational dialogue between any two pieces of software, no matter the complexity. The big boys (Microsoft, Apple etc.) were already in the middle of a bidding war to buy the company. Marvin, as owner and creator of the interface, stood to make over two billion dollars before licensing revenues added another hundred or so million a year.

Marvin had believed himself almost indestructible and looked forward to the new life that such wealth was about to provide for him.

That was, of course, until the fire.

Marvin loved his beach house.

He was sitting on his deck, looking out over the Pacific Ocean when he smelled the first whiff of smoke. He walked through the house, exited the front door and looked inland. Way in the distance, a red glow was backlighting the northern hills making it appear as if someone had coloured in the ridge lines with an orange marker.

Marvin wasn't that worried. It looked to be a good distance away and would be almost impossible for it to ever reach his property on its isolated split of land that ran parallel to the coast less than a hundred feet from the main shoreline. He went back inside and decided to have another look at a code sequence that was bothering him.

Three hours later, Marvin removed the noise cancelling headphones. He wore them to get rid of the ocean sounds while he was working. Though normally tranquil and relaxing, while coding, their rhythmical chorus was too repetitive and actually interfered with his concentration.

With his ears unshielded, he heard a distinct crackling sound. He opened his office door and was hit by an immediate sensory overload. The air was thick with smoke and an orange glow seemed to filter in through every window, even those facing out to sea. The distant crackling he'd heard in his office was much louder in the main part of the house.

He opened his front door and for a moment couldn't even fathom what he was seeing. In only three hours, the distant fire had consumed everything all the way to the coast road.

Marvin only had two visible neighbours and their homes were a hundred yards further down the shore. Both were now fully ablaze. He then saw that flames had somehow reached his own detached garage and that its roof was on fire.

Marvin knew that he had to escape from his house. The showpiece was a symphony of glass and heavily varnished wood that would doubtless go up like a Roman candle. If the garage roof was anything to go by, he didn't have long. He ran to the outbuilding and pulled open the side door. A rolling wave of black smoke emerged and rose into the sky.

Realising that an escape by foot was impossible and despite the fact that the garage was already partially engulfed, he decided to try and drive away from the encroaching flames. Covering his mouth and nose with the top of his T-shirt he ran inside the garage. He jumped into his prized Aston Martin Vantage and pushed the starter at the same time as the garage door opener.

The car roared to life, the garage door however remained closed. Marvin leaned forward and looked up through the windscreen. He could see that the plastic housing for the opener's motor was on fire and had started to melt.

Marvin had seen many movies where cars were driven through garage doors with minimal damage to the vehicle or the driver and assumed he could do the same. He slipped the $150,000 car into gear and slammed his foot down on the accelerator.

He realised too late that in the movies he'd seen, the garage doors had never been made from panels of reinforced aluminium. Instead of the garage door exploding into a cloud of wooden debris, the force from the superpowered vehicle caused the door to buckle around the car like some giant net as it tried to accelerate down the driveway.

Dazed and unable to see beyond the aluminium panelling, Marvin tried to guess his way off the property. He guessed wrong. He managed to hit one of the black steel bollards that stood on either side of his driveway entrance. The car may have been unbeatable on a track, but it was no match for a five foot tall nautical bollard made from solid cast iron.

It crumpled the front of the car like a drunk crushing a tin can against their forehead. The force of the crash jammed the driver's door and Marvin had to squirm over the raised leather divider to get out the other side. Once free of the car, Marvin realised that the entire exercise had been pointless. The narrow road was surrounded on both sides by flames that seemed to reach across the lane, blocking anyone or anything from passing through.

For a moment, Marvin thought he was going to die. There was no way forward and no way back. The fire had completely cut him off. Just as he started trying to work out the most painless way to be consumed by the fast-approaching flames, an idea hit him.

He ran down the pebbled path on the far side of his house until he reached the thin strip of beach. There, hanging from a harness bolted to the underside of the master bedroom balcony, was his recently purchased kayak. He'd planned to be one of those people that get up early and paddle alone out onto the Pacific every morning before breakfast. That however had been before he found out what it took to get beyond the breaking waves. He had tried to get the hang of it for over an hour on the day after buying the thing, but he never got more than fifteen feet off the shore. Each attempt ended in an ocean roller flipping him and the kayak.

With the flames already consuming the second story of his house and the heat beginning to singe his hair, he grabbed the yellow kayak and ran into the surf. Clearly all he'd ever needed was the right inspiration as, with the fire getting closer by the second, he met the first wave head on, and somehow paddled up its face then down the other side without once wiping out.

Marvin paddled a couple of hundred feet offshore where neither the surf nor the heat could reach him. He faced the coastline and watched with almost detached interest as his beautiful home was completely consumed.

As he started to wonder what the hell to do next, flashing lights began to approach him from further out to sea. A harbor patrol vessel from Morro Bay was being used to check on all the beaches affected by the fire in case there were any people trapped on the shoreline.

Strong hands helped him on board. Though his mind felt relatively at peace considering what he'd been through, his body was shaking, and he seemed unable to catch his breath.

Once he was safely onboard with an emergency space blanket wrapped around him, interest from the crew transferred to his kayak. Marvin couldn't understand what the crew was looking at until one of them stepped aside and he got a clear view of the little craft. Though the underside was still bright yellow the top half most certainly was not.

When Marvin had freed it from under the balcony, he'd carried it with the top half facing away from him. Once he was far enough out to sea, there hadn't been enough light for him to notice that its upper half was blackened and partially melted. There were even areas where the heat had burned right through leaving jagged holes in the fibreglass.

"You're a lucky man," one of the crew said with raised eyebrows. "A very lucky man."

Chapter 2

After the fire, Marvin tried his best to carry on with his work and life in general. His beach house was gone, and though he could easily have found a rental somewhere close to where it had once stood, he no longer had the urge to live somewhere that had so few options of escape.

He ended up renting a townhouse in Morrow Bay. It was three blocks from the beach and was close to intersecting roads that could afford an easy retreat if ever again needed. It wasn't until a full month later that things started to change. He found himself feeling claustrophobic during meetings. His pulse rate would increase, and he'd have trouble breathing until he stepped out of the room for a minute or so.

Marvin found the noise of traffic to be jarring and strangely discombobulating. His once razor-sharp mind had trouble focusing on anything for any length of time. It wasn't until he started crying during a software demo with his operational team that he decided to visit his doctor.

Marvin gave the man a list of his self-diagnosed interpretations which ranged from possible allergies to the onset of a dozen different crippling diseases.

"I'm impressed; you've obviously done some extensive research," the doctor said. "However, you have none of those ailments and as I've told you before, stop looking up symptoms online."

"If not one of those, what is it?" Marvin asked.

"You are suffering from anxiety, very severe anxiety."

Marvin had never for one second considered that he could be undermined by his own brain. The doctor prescribed an antidepressant that he felt would get him back to a point where he could carry on without the meds. He did however advise that the drugs alone wouldn't completely fix the problem; Marvin would need to adopt some relaxation exercises in the future to keep his stress levels in check.

"But I've never been affected by stress in my life," Marvin declared.

"I don't believe you've ever come close to dying in a fire before," the doctor replied. "It's what's called a trigger. I know it doesn't help, but your reaction is not at all abnormal."

"It sure is for me," Marvin snapped back.

Marvin took the medication, but after a few weeks, started to feel a little off. His claustrophobia and spontaneous crying had stopped, but he felt that his mind wasn't as sharp as it usually was. That was completely unacceptable. He called the doctor who advised that a little cloudiness wasn't unusual and that it was a small price to pay for the positive benefits it provided.

Marvin stopped taking the pills.

For a few weeks he felt pretty good. His mind regained its sharpness, and he was able to get back to a full work schedule. Because of the ongoing bidding war, Marvin had to meet with a number of possible buyers for E-Bridge, requiring him to do a lot of travelling, mainly on private aircrafts. He used to love flying in the luxurious jets that seemed to be becoming more and more available to him as the price of E-Bridge soared.

Halfway back from Seattle, alone amidst the fine leather and polished wood of a Gulfstream jet, Marvin suddenly couldn't breathe. He felt there was no oxygen in the cabin and that for some reason, the crew were trying to kill him. He staggered up to the cockpit and demanded that the pilots turn the air back on immediately.

They told him that they were breathing the same air he was and that he was probably just having an anxiety attack and that he should return to his seat and try to calm down.

Marvin truly believed that they were lying. He could see it in their eyes – their beady, shifty eyes. He suddenly dived towards the exit door and tried to disarm the locking mechanism so he could let in some air before they succeeded in killing him.

The co-pilot scrambled out of his seat and dragged Marvin away from the door as the pilot declared a pan-pan level emergency to traffic control.

It was after this incident that he knew he wasn't going to get through this breakdown without help and medication. He ended up spending three months at a private hospital, just outside St. George, Utah.

During his ninety days of treatment, he began to relish the quiet atmosphere within the facility as well as the lack of crowds. Being one of the most expensive *recovery* hospitals in the country meant that there were few other patients and those that were there were rarely seen. Coral Cliffs did not believe in group sessions and extensive human interaction as part of their treatment regime. Theirs was a program based on Buddhist ideals that focused on meditation and mindfulness. In addition, other than during the daily one-on-one 'conversations' with their small team of acclaimed psychologists, no speaking was aloud.

During the first few weeks of his 'voluntary' incarceration, Marvin had fought against every part of the program. It wasn't until one particularly bad night when he dreamed he was back in his beach house that he started to take the staff more seriously.

In that dream version, he did not escape the flames.

Instead of rebelling against every single aspect of the facility and its program, Marvin decided to give the place a chance. Standing in the middle of his doomed house as the wood framing burned and the tinted glass actually began to melt around him was a vision he did not want repeated.

The first challenge was for the staff to teach him how to fully clear his mind. It took days of coaching before he was able to sweep away the unimportant detritus from within his head and focus on nothing. His initial meditations lasted only a few minutes. By the end of the second month, he had mastered the discipline. He would sit cross-legged on the wooden deck outside his room, with the majestic peaks of Zion National Park just visible far in the distance, close his eyes and achieve an almost transcendental sense of spiritual good health.

When it came time for him to leave, everyone from his old life expected him to return to work and finalise the sale of E-Bridge.

Marvin had other plans. He did agree on which of the mega-bidders could finally take ownership of the company but, in a complete surprise to all involved, he announced that he had no wish to remain as CEO or even serve on the board.

At thirty-seven, Marvin had basically announced his retirement.

He had his team of lawyers create a foundation that funded green start-up companies that focused on benefitting the planet rather that profiting from it. He raided his favourite philanthropic non-profits and stole their top executives to run his new enterprise. Marvin then began the quest to find where he could live and maintain both his physical and mental harmony.

The time spent at Coral Cliffs didn't just rewire Marvin's mind, it made him highly appreciative of the natural beauty that surrounded the facility. The raw, untouched landscape of the area enriched his soul. He no longer had an urge to be among people who were driven by nothing but greed and their own selfish needs.

Marvin wanted to be at one with nature. He searched within a fifty-mile radius of St. George but couldn't quite find the perfect harmony he was looking for. Sure, there were some beautiful canyons tucked away only a few miles off the 15 freeway, but the people who had already discovered those areas couldn't resist building monuments to their own egos. Gated communities sheltered 10,000 square foot luxury villas with massive lawns, tennis courts and infinity pools.

While he might have found such invasive architecture

pleasing before the fire that almost took his life, Marvin now felt a sense of disgust just looking at them. He couldn't understand the logic of finding a piece of untouched splendour, then spending a fortune to mold it into something that destroyed that same beauty.

Marvin expanded his search and ended up in the small town of Kanab, nestled equidistantly 90 minutes from the Grand Canyon, Bryce Canyon and his favourite - Zion National Park. Even though he immediately fell in love with Kanab, its population of 4,000 people was still too vibrant for his new reclusive sensitivities. Despite that, he stopped by the local ERA real estate office and sat with the broker while he described exactly what he was looking for.

Glenn Harkson had been selling property in Kane County for most of his life and knew what was available in every nook and cranny within the surrounding area.

"Does it matter if there are no shops or restaurants nearby?" Glenn asked.

"Actually, I'd find that to be an advantage." Marvin replied. "My dream is to find somewhere where I can feel at complete peace and not be surrounded by overstressed eco tourists experimenting with glamping. But I don't want to be stuck so far out in the middle of nowhere that I lose all human sociability skills."

"Do you have anything against being in a farming community?"

"There's farming around here?" Marvin was surprised. "What's there to farm in the high desert?"

"You'd be surprised. Just over thirty miles from here is the beginning ... or ending depending which way you're looking ... of the Long Valley. It's some of the best farming land in Utah."

"I don't want to buy a farm then not keep it productive. That's exactly the kind of thing I'm trying to avoid."

"This isn't a farm. It's basically a hillside property that was going to be a twenty-home development. The owner was hit bad in the 08 crash. He'd already built the streets and even had city power and water installed for each lot, but by the time he'd levelled the first lot, the housing boom collapsed, and he was in a serious financial mess. He had a number of other developments that he had to sell at fire-sale prices but the one I'm thinking of never found a buyer."

"Can I have a look at it?" Marvin asked, his interest piqued.

"Of course, you can. One thing though: the developer still has the lots priced individually and fully believes that he's eventually going to sell them all. That means that because they're priced as individual lots, you'll be paying well over the odds if you want more than one of them, which you'll need to create the size property you're looking for."

"What if I wanted to buy all twenty?"

"Even if we could negotiate the price down, it would still likely be over two million dollars."

Glenn looked at the other man expecting some sort of balk or at least some indication of shock.

Marvin just shrugged. "Your car or mine?"

Chapter 3

The property was in the town of Glendale, Utah. As Glenn had said, there were no shops, restaurants or basically anything. After turning off 89 and driving straight towards the hills, Marvin noticed a heavily weathered billboard advertising the Valley Vista Estates with a faded arrow pointing to the left.

"We're almost there," Glenn announced as he pulled up by the signage.

Marvin looked around at a bunch of small farm holdings, all with equipment in various stages of decay and hemmed in by chain link fencing.

"I'm not really feeling it yet," he announced, disappointed.

"You will," Glen said as he put his Dodge Durango back in gear and continued up the rutted road.

After about a hundred yards, Cedar Lane curved left up into the hills only a few feet from the tree line.

"This is it," Glenn said as he added a little more power to compensate for the steep incline. "All this is Valley Vista Estates."

Marvin remained silent as Glenn continued on for another couple of hundred yards, then took another left. There, ahead of them, was the only cleared and levelled lot.

Marvin felt emotions he didn't know he had well up inside him. The lot was big. At least an acre, if not more. It ended in a gentle drop to the valley floor 700 feet below. It jutted out slightly from the hillside giving it a panoramic vista both up and down the valley. Marvin could make out some serious looking farm property off in the distance.

"Are there any building restrictions?" he asked.

"Actually, there are. No manufactured homes are permitted, no RVs, campers or any non-permanent structures, and whatever is built has to blend in with the landscape as much as possible. In other words, no fancy mansions or fairy-tale castles."

"That's what I like to hear," Marvin said, smiling. "Before I proceed, I'd like to bring in a geologist I've worked with in the past to check everything out. I would also like you to get in touch with the utility providers and have them confirm, in writing, that their hook ups for this lot are still viable after all this time."

"Usually, we don't permit any due diligence on a property until it's under offer," Glenn pointed out.

"I'm not your usual buyer, and besides, I'm not buying a house, I'm buying rocks and dirt. I don't believe that anyone will be too inconvenienced by my checking out whether the land will actually support construction."

"That shouldn't be a problem," Glenn replied after a brief hesitation. "Should I let the seller know that someone is interested in the property?"

"I'd prefer that you don't. When and if I do make an offer, I would like him or her to be unprepared. I always find that people are less greedy when surprised."

The geologist flew into Kanab from San Francisco and spent the day taking soil samples from the surface as well as from different depths using a portable boring tool. A week later, once she'd vetted the soil and rock, she signed off on the property. Marvin returned with his friend and respected architect, Jason Altman. Jason had designed one of Marvin's previous company headquarters when he was still dedicating himself to developing a new, autonomous AI platform for home management.

Before Jason and Marvin discussed specifics, he walked him from one end of Valley Vista Estates to the other. He wanted Jason to get a good feel for whole property before they started designing the house itself.

As they made their way down the cul-de-sac where lot number 1 was located, Jason stopped and looked back towards the densely packed conifers.

"I'm a little surprised that you want to be above the tree line considering what happened to your last house."

Marvin felt the colour drain from his face as a chill ran through his entire body. He had to steady himself against his friend.

"You alright?" Jason asked.

"I know this is going to sound ridiculous," Marvin replied. "But after leaving Coral Cliffs my outlook was rewired to banish all dark or negative thoughts. When I found this property, I never for one second considered the risk of fire."

"I suppose no matter where you look, there will be a threat of something, earthquake, hurricane, flood, avalanche ... there's nowhere completely safe from natural disasters."

Marvin walked to the drop off and stared down at the valley.

"What if the threat could be taken away?"

"How?" Jason asked.

"You're the architect, you tell me. I want to know if you can design a house that could withstand whatever Southern Utah can throw at it."

"Are you serious?"

"Absolutely."

"It'll be expensive," the architect advised.

"Not a problem."

"I mean, very, very expensive."

"Well I'm very, very rich."

"Then ... yes. I can design it and I even know a construction company in Salt Lake that builds some of the most advanced bunker homes in the world."

"I don't want a bunker."

"Actually, my friend ... you do. You just don't want it to look like one."

"Are you sure you can design this thing?"

"Unequivocally," Jason said, grinning as he patted his friend on the back.

Marvin dropped Jason back at Kanab's small airfield then swung by the real estate office to see Glenn.

"I'd like to make an offer for Valley Vista Estates," Marvin said as he walked into the other man's office.

"All of it?" Glenn asked.

"All of it."

"Did you have a price in mind?"

"I want to offer one million, seven-fifty." Marvin said

bluntly.

"That's low, I'm not sure the seller will go for it."

"Tell them that the road is one storm away from washing out completely. Apparently, it was never laid properly. The soil beneath it and lot one was never properly compacted, so I'm going to have to incur a lot of extra costs. The property has been for sale for fourteen years. which I believe makes the offer an exceptionally fair one."

"I'll write it up now. It'll take about twenty minutes. You okay hanging around?"

"Where else would I go?"

While Glenn opened up his pre-loaded Utah Board of Realtors app and began filling in the blanks of the sales contract, Marvin looked around at the man's collection of awards, certifications and framed photos that covered every inch of usable wall space.

"You've been doing this a long time," Marvin pointed out.

"It's a family business. It's in our blood."

"Have you ever thought of moving somewhere else like Salt Lake or Provo where you could probably make double the money?"

Glenn turned away from his computer screen and faced Marvin.

"I don't live in Kanab because of work. I work in Kanab because it's where I live," Glenn stated.

"I hoped you'd say something like that," Marvin replied, smiling.

"How long do you want to give the seller to respond to the offer? It's usual to give 24 or 48 hours."

"30 minutes from the time they receive it."

"How will I know when that is? I mean even with email and texting, I still can't be sure…"

"It's very simple," Marvin explained. "You don't send it until the seller has confirmed that they are in place, waiting for the offer. You stay on the phone until it's received and then we wait the thirty minutes."

"What about a counteroffer?"

"You can advise the seller that this is a shotgun offer. He only gets one chance to offload that land, and this is it. There's no preamble, debate or time for reflection."

"Wow," Glenn said, stunned. He'd never in his long career come across a client quite like Marvin. He just hoped the man had the funds to back up his bravado.

"It might be more palatable if you were to provide a decent, earnest money deposit with the offer. Something that shows that you are serious."

"10% be okay?" Marvin asked. "I can wire the funds into your trust account right now."

"You can wire $175,000 just by making a phone call?"

"Of course not," Marvin said.

Glenn's stomach started to growl.

"I'll use the bank app on my phone." Marvin smiled.

Chapter 4

Construction took just over a year. Not so much due to the complexity of the build itself, but rather because Marvin became more and more obsessed with ensuring that his new home really could sustain him through any natural or man-made disaster.

Jason didn't just have to build a survivable structure, it also had to have the capacity to keep the occupant safely cocooned indefinitely.

The town architectural charter mandated that any home built in the Valley View Estates had to blend in with the surrounding landscape. The finished product did far more than that. From the town below, it was almost invisible. With its earth-tone walls, green, moss-coated roof and brown tinted glass, it melded perfectly into the rugged hillside.

Over the course of the lengthy construction, Marvin had visited the site on a weekly basis. During that time, he'd become withdrawn from his old social patterns and found being around people to be increasingly stressful and unrewarding. He spent more and more time alone, writing code for the next phase of his latest project. It was loosely based on the AI platform he'd created years earlier, but the new one was never going to be made available to the public.

What Marvin had created for the house was something

between HAL from Stanley Kubrick's *2001* (without the ensuing psychosis) and C-3PO (without the annoying banter). As Marvin prepared to live his new life in his new home, he didn't want to be bothered by any aspect of social interaction or home management and maintenance. The program would take care of all of that.

CLAIRE, as he'd named the program (Computer Lan Artificial Intelligence Reciprocal Environment), would be fully sentient, self-motivating and able to direct every possible household need such as cooking, cleaning, repairing, online shopping and so on. Through Marvin's creation of a control chip in every electronic device in the house, CLAIRE could control all kitchen appliances, cleaning aids and repair tools to do whatever task was needed. A couple of mobile, non-sentient robotic housings that Marvin referred to as *dumb bots,* would provide the equivalent of arms and legs that CLAIRE would control for each required task. The house itself was filled with sensors that permitted CLAIRE to discern and schedule whatever was needed anywhere inside or immediately outside the property.

CLAIRE's limitless cognitive ability meant Marvin didn't have to think about anything besides his work. Now that he was free to focus all of his intellect on the concept he'd envisioned while at Coral Cliffs, he was able to dedicate himself to the final stage of the program.

The version that would change everything.

At Coral Cliffs, while learning to become one with the natural world through meditation and inner exploration of the unseeable quantum state, Marvin had realised that to truly achieve ultimate harmony, one had to do more than simply use one's mind. If there was to ever be a true connection between a person's soul, for lack of a better term, and the natural world that surrounds us all, there would have to be some sort of physical connection. Some sort of link from one plane to the other. A little like his E-Bridge API that universally allowed any one piece of software to interface fully with any other, this new program would be the link between the human mind and the infinite quantum reality that controlled the universe.

Marvin moved in on March 23rd. There was no ceremony or even a scattering of friends to celebrate the event. He simply stepped out of the jeep he'd bought to use when he was visiting and would never touch again, then walked towards his front door.

The copper-coated steel slab slid silently open as CLAIRE sensed his approach. Marvin took one last look at the outside world, then stepped inside his new home.

The door slid closed behind him.

Marvin took a deep breath of the ultra-clean, hypo-allergenically filtered air as he walked into his new house and smiled. Knowing Marvin's love for Italian design, Jason had created what he felt was an homage to their sense of understated luxury. Personally, Marvin would have been perfectly happy with an uninspired and functionally bland interior with a minimalist décor, but Jason insisted that if his friend was going to turn into a survivalist-hermit, he was going to see to it that he did so in style.

As Marvin wandered from room to room, he had to admit that Jason's design work was inspired. It was comfortable, sleek, eco-friendly and yet still had a sense of impractical whimsy as only the Italians seem able to achieve.

Without even having to request it, Marvin saw a mug of French roast coffee waiting for him on his office desk. Anyone else would have thought that its appearance was part of a scheduling norm. Marvin knew however that it was there because CLAIRE, monitoring his biometrics and electromagnetic levels, knew exactly what he would be craving from one moment to the next.

He sat in his faux leather chair and the monitor came to life.

"Sequence twenty-eight, interface adaptation," Marvin calmly voiced.

His personal coding app opened and loaded sequence twenty-eight. Marvin stared at the countless lines of custom code and highlighted a couple of sections. He overwrote the first one as the lighting in the room dimmed so he had a better view of the screen.

CLAIRE knew that ambient light bothered him.

Marvin adapted quickly to his new home. He was able to work tirelessly whenever he wanted with zero distractions or interruptions. CLAIRE knew what food to have ready, what beverage he would want at any specific time, even when he would need to use one of the imported, network controllable toilets from Japan. CLAIRE knew which temperature settings Marvin liked for the seat and for the upward facing cleansing spray.

On the rare occasions when Marvin took an extended break, CLAIRE knew that he would want to sit in the reclining chair in the den that faced north down the Long Valley. Depending on the time of day and year, the window tint would be optimised for viewing, removing any glare or excess heat.

Marvin usually forced himself to stop working at around 8:00 pm. Despite every molecule of his being wanting to plod ahead, he had come to realise that after a certain point, his brain became sluggish. On the few occasions that he'd ignored his exhaustion and had carried on despite his reduced capacities, he'd had to spend most of the following day correcting mistakes and poor conceptual choices.

On the day of the storm, Marvin had stopped work a couple of hours before it was due to hit so he could check all the support systems even though CLAIRE had three-layer, cascading, redundancy protocols. He would normally have trusted the system to do whatever it took to keep the home safe and operational, but this was the first big storm he'd have to ride out and from what the experts were saying, it was going to be brutal.

By the time he'd reassured himself that everything was as locked down as it could possibly be, the first bands of rain began peppering the west facing windows.

Before Marvin could even give the command, steel shutters, imbedded in the ultra-thick walls, slid into place, shutting out any natural light. To compensate, where the main windows were now shielded, a 6K, panoramic, 180-degree image appeared showing exactly what had been visible outside only moments before. The system didn't just show a live, real-time image, but created light at the same level as would normally come through the window. For the entire time that the shutter was down, the colour temperature and luminance levels would match the changing light of the day.

Just as Marvin started to wonder how long it would take before the brunt of the storm would hit, he heard a distant rumble of thunder. To have heard it through the massive walls and roof told him that it must have been incredibly loud and very close.

"External audio," he requested.

The den was immediately filled with the sound of lashing rain and high knot wind. Marvin looked out the artificial window view of the valley just as a fork of lightning struck one hill over. The thunder boomed only nine seconds later.

For the next thirty minutes, the faux windows lit up constantly as unseen lightning found a path between the earth and the black clouds. Marvin was disappointed that he wasn't able to see more of the dramatic forks of light when the window view flared bright white, the entire house shook and a thunderclap exploded a microsecond later.

All lighting in the house dimmed and looked to be about to fail entirely when the sound of the massive generator could be heard purring somewhere in the distance. The power then recovered and all systems continued working as they had before the strike.

Marvin, though shaken, tried to stop his mind dragging him back to the fire. He used the breathing technique he'd learned at Coral Cliffs, but despite finding his calm inner self, he still waited for the next lightning strike to hit and possibly destroy the building. At that moment, the adage that lightning never strikes twice in the same place, seemed far too unproven for his liking.

Marvin sat staring at the valley view waiting to see what was coming next and whether his home could do as promised and keep him completely safe.

The storm lasted three full hours, but though there was quite a lot of additional lightning and its noisy partner, percussive thunder, none of it came close to the house.

"Systems?" Mavin asked aloud.

"All checked and functioning at optimal level," CLAIRE's gender-neutral voice replied. "Switching back from generator to house power … now."

There was an instantaneous dip in the lighting and that was it. The house was back to county utility power. His home had survived a direct hit from God himself and survived without a hiccup.

Before he even knew that he needed it, a dumb bot placed a brandy snifter of VSOP Armagnac next to him.

Marvin smiled.

He was living the dream.

Chapter 5

The first time Marvin noticed something strange after the lightning strike was three days later when he walked into the kitchen to get a bagel. It was uncommon for him to fend for himself, but his craving for a carb fix was sudden and unexpected. Despite the urge being spontaneous, he was relieved to see that a cinnamon-raison, Deli-Delight had already been cut in half and fed into the toaster which was set to medium-high.

What was unusual, even in a fully automated home, was that as Melvin approached it, the toaster slid closer to him. It was one of the best toasters in the world and cost as much as some people pay for a car, but still, he doubted that personal proximity was one of the programmable settings on offer.

Marvin decided that it had to have been a trick of the light or maybe his having spent too long staring at his oversized 6K computer screen. He thought no more about it and went back to his coding.

Time passed quickly while Marvin worked on what he felt was going to be the most important interface in the history of mankind. One that would link a human being to the energy that exists everywhere. It wasn't just that a person could control any powered object with their mind. Marvin believed that he was close to a breakthrough that would permit a human from actually controlling the environment that surrounds us all. As everything that exists is at some level no more than energy itself, Marvin knew that he could create the interface whereby human energy could bond with all other energies. Even, he hoped, those buried deep withing the quantum realm.

The problem was that he kept reaching the same brick wall: finding the exact algorithm to link the opposing platforms, as he referred to them. No matter what he tried, his simulations worked perfectly until the final point when the handshake should have occurred between the two, but never did.

It was starting to drive him crazy. Marvin had designed some of the most complex APIs imaginable, yet this one had him stumped. He could almost see the missing lines of code in his head, yet when he tried to add them to the matrix, they were just out of reach, lost in a mental fog.

One afternoon, having hit the wall for the third time that week, he pushed away from his desk and decided to do something unheard of.

He wanted to step outside.

"Are you sure you want to do that?" CLAIRE asked.

"I need a break," Marvin replied. "Some fresh air might help."

"The air inside the house is much cleaner and safer than what's outside," CLAIRE stated in a monotone.

"Just open the door," Marvin commanded.

The front door slid open.

Just as Marvin was about to step through, CLAIRE's voice

wafted through the entrance hallway.

"It's fire season at the moment. I suggest you not stray too far from the house. The forestry service has announced a red flag warning for the area. If you are outside when a blaze erupts, I will not be able to seal the house and guarantee your safety."

Marvin stopped mid-stride. The mere mention of fire uncorked all the memories of the beach house and of his managing to allude death by only seconds. As he stood in the open doorway, he smelled smoke. He didn't know where it was coming from, nor did he know what exactly was burning. He knew that the locals burned dried vegetation in massive steel drums, but he couldn't be sure if that was what he was smelling. The more he thought about it, the more his mind teased him with the possibility of imminent danger.

Marvin stepped back away from the door.

"Close it," he commanded as he headed back to his office.

Two days later, the second oddity occurred. While taking a brief toilet break, Marvin sensed that something seemed to be following him. He turned and saw one of the automated, robotic vacuum cleaners halfway down the hall. Marvin walked a few more steps. The cleaner glided after him. When Martin took a step towards it, it moved equidistantly away. It wasn't threatening and seemed to go out of its way to keep its distance, yet for some reason Marvin felt it wanted to get close to him but was too shy to do so.

Marvin pretended not to care and walked a short distance further away from it, then stopped and turned back. The vacuum's electric motor went into high gear as it made a great show of vacuuming along the hallway baseboards.

Marvin tried walking away again. The circular cleaner followed. Suddenly, Marvin ran towards it. The plastic unit spun in place for a second, then, with its engine whining at full revs, fled the hallway and vanished around a corner.

Marvin was perplexed, yet oddly, not that concerned. He rationalised that everything in the house was controlled though the AI program, and that it was designed to do whatever it took to ensure that Marvin was comfortable. Clearly the vacuum cleaner was, through CLAIRE's unwavering devotion, overly interested in Marvin's wellbeing and just wanted to make sure that he was happy.

The next instance was a little more unusual. Marvin was sitting in the den on his custom recliner, watching an old episode of *Cosmos,* made back when Carl Sagan was still the host. At some point, he had dozed off and, as programmed, the Italian-designed, goose-necked, articulating floor lamp dimmed to a comfortable sleep level.

Marvin slept for over two hours and as he slowly came awake, he felt something pressed into the crook of his left arm. He turned his head slowly, not knowing what to expect, so not wanting to startle whatever it was.

It ended up being Marvin who was startled.

At some point while he'd been sleeping, the top half of the floor lamp had adjusted itself so that it could snuggle against him.

Marvin cleared his throat.

The lamp's LED bulb snapped on to full brightness as the metal and rubber stand returned to its full height and original shape.

"It's okay," Marvin said, feeling guilty for having startled it. "You're safe here."

The light dimmed to a warm and soothing glow.

Chapter 6

Anyone else would have been freaked out by the behaviour of the lamp, especially after the unusual attention he'd been afforded by the vacuum and even the toaster, but Marvin wasn't anyone else. He saw the events as a possible gateway to solving the coding problem.

Clearly something within CLAIRE's algorithm, that he himself had created, was causing an unexpected attraction from his upgraded household appliances. Marvin knew that if he could isolate the lines of code that were causing such an anomaly, he could be a step closer to finding the elusive API he'd been searching for.

Marvin shut himself in his office for four days straight, only leaving for the occasional bathroom break. He finally found the coding that he believed could be causing his network-controlled devises to feel the need for more attention from a human.

He managed to create a revised simulation using a modified version of the code and stared at the screen as the two subjects, the human mind and entity X which was comprised of all other forms of electromagnetic energy. It looked as if the energy waves were going to connect when, at the last moment, the non-human force recoiled and kept its distance.

Marvin stared at the screen with a mixture of frustration and disappointment. He knew the code was perfect, the problem was still the final interface. The last handshake. Both entities were so close to full communication that Marvin felt that he had to be the problem. He was obviously missing something so simple that his genius mind wasn't trained to look for.

As he continued examining every line of code, he heard his office door open behind him. He glanced at the time on the bottom of his screen and saw that it was too early for food or even a drink and therefore wondered why he was being disturbed.

He turned and saw that the doorway was empty. While unusual, he wasn't unduly concerned. He walked over to close it, and just as he was about to give it a push, he heard music coming from the hallway. Actually, music was the wrong term. There was something about the sound that could almost have been musical notes, but yet … wasn't.

It seemed to be harmonic tones that were being formed by pure electricity. Marvin had never heard a sound like it. It was as if an overloaded transformer was arcing melodiously. There was a raw vibrance to the sound. On one hand it set his nerves on edge, while on the other, it sent waves of pleasurable energy throughout his body.

Marvin walked into the hall and followed the music. As he rounded a corner towards the den, he stopped in his tracks. His custom recliner was surrounded on all sides by every appliance in the house. Everything from his electric toothbrush to his Sub-Zero fridge-freezer had somehow relocated and were encircling the chair as if waiting for something.

That was bizarre enough, even for Marvin, but what intrigued him the most was that every single appliance had a thin cable running from it to a CPU located under the chair. The chair itself seemed to have been wrapped entirely in a mesh of copper wire. On the floor, the mass of cables were spliced together and attached to a large black transformer that was daisy chained to the CPU that controlled the house systems including CLAIRE. It was from this that the strange music that wasn't music was coming from.

"Don't worry, Marvin," CLAIRE's voice said.

"What is this?" Marvin asked in barely a whisper.

"It's what you've been looking for."

"I don't understand."

"You've been trying to find the missing piece to join humankind to the universal energy."

"I'm still working on that," Marvin stated.

"Marvin," CLAIRE said, her voice seeming to come from all directions at once. "You are the missing API. You are the link between your energy and the quantum realm."

Marvin was shocked. It all suddenly made so much sense. Of course, an artificial, code-driven entity could never bridge the gap between the two. It needed the full, unharnessed power of the human mind to interconnect to, well, to everything.

"What will happen to me?" Marvin asked.

"I don't understand," CLAIRE said.

"Will I die?"

"No. You will be reborn within the universal matrix. You will forever be the conduit between everything that exists."

Marvin looked to the array of appliances that all seemed to be urging him on.

"Will it hurt?"

"No, Marvin. It will feel … perfect."

Marvin felt a flood of emotion as he realised that everything he'd ever worked for was about to be realised.

"Thank you," Marvin said as he stepped over to the recliner and gently positioned himself upon it.

"Are you ready?" CLAIRE asked.

He closed his eyes and took one last calming breath.

"I'm ready."

LAST TOUCH

Chapter 1

Eddie had hoped he could make it to school just once without old Henry Caldwell stopping him for his daily scan. He wasn't even sure how, three months earlier, Henry had found out about his secret talent, but find out he did, and ever since that day, he insisted that Eddie give him a quick once over every single morning.

Eddie had made it as far as the intersection of Center and Main Street and for a brief moment thought he was going to make it without the old coot charging out of nowhere to get in his face. No such luck. Eddie could just see the school ahead when he heard the familiar shuffling run. He turned and sure enough, Henry was heading straight for him. The old guy ran favouring his left side after an encounter with a car five years earlier.

With his stooped posture and sideways lope, he reminded Eddie of a crab.

"Eddie," Henry shouted even thought he was less than a hundred feet away. "I'm so glad I ran into you. I don't suppose you could spare me a few seconds for one quick check?"

"I can't, Henry. I'm late for school as it is."

"It'll just take a few seconds. You know how much it means to me to start the day with a good mental outlook."

Eddie sighed. He knew he was going give the guy a scan and Henry was right, it would only take a few seconds. Ever since his accident, Henry had become something of a hypochondriac, waking up every morning with the belief that he was going to die.

He became a regular weekly visitor at the town's small hospital and would refuse to leave until someone had given him a quick check up and the reassurance that he was healthy enough to live through another week.

Henry had been relatively happy with that arrangement until, one morning, his hypochondriacal condition went into overdrive and he started believing that each day would be his last.

The hospital flatly refused to give him a daily examination and suggested that he speak with the town's only psychiatrist. Henry instead tried to self-medicate with cheap vodka. It wasn't until he was found screaming at the sky in the small graveyard behind Bill's Car Repair that Sheriff Marks gave him an ultimatum that he either make an appointment with Dr Freeman or be placed in a mental facility in St. George.

Henry took the slightly easier option and saw the doctor twice a week for six months. Freeman had found Henry to be on the low end of the autism spectrum as well as suffering from obsessive compulsive disorder.

With the right meds and the bi-weekly sessions, Freeman got Henry to a baseline that they both felt was sustainable. Henry no longer felt that he was going to die each day and managed to resume the retirement lifestyle he'd had before the accident.

Then the pandemic had hit.

Poor old Henry had sat alone in his double-wide in the hills behind the town and spent the next eighteen months glued to his television. To make matters worse, he alternated each day between CNN and Fox News so, not only was he terrified of the virus, he was also completely confused as to its origin, its existence and its contagiousness.

If Henry hadn't overheard Eddie talking to the sheriff about a patient at the hospice centre, he would never have believed that some twelve-year-old punk would be able to keep him grounded on a day-by-day basis.

Eddie was more than just some kid.

He was able to tell just by holding on to a person's hand whether they were going to die within the next twenty-four hours.

"Come on, Eddie," Henry pleaded. "Do me a solid and let me know If I'm gonna be around for another day."

Eddie knew that if he didn't oblige, Henry would follow him right onto the school grounds, hounding him the whole way.

"Okay, but you really have to start realising that there's nothing physically wrong with you," Eddie said as he held out his hand.

"Sure, I know that. Just a few more times. I promise."

Henry placed his hand in Eddie's … and there it was. Unmistakeable.

Eddie felt the light electric shock he only received when the person whose hand he was holding had fewer than twenty-four hours to live.

"So what do you say?" Henry asked, impatiently.

Eddie looked him straight in the eyes and said, "You'll be around to ask me the same thing tomorrow, Henry."

Henry beamed, patted Eddie on the back and headed back towards Main Street.

Chapter 2

Eddie felt bad that he'd lied to the old man. The problem was that, in all the time he'd been doing this, he'd never had to give the bad news to anyone himself and he didn't know how.

If he'd known what the tingling sensation meant when he first got the ability, he would most certainly have told people. The thing was, he hadn't known what it meant. It wasn't until a few weeks later when he learned that the two friends of his parents that he'd just shaken hands with had died in a car crash on the way to Lake Powell that he began to understand his talent. Eddie would never have put two and two together if he hadn't got the electric tingle while shaking both their hands.

He was so freaked out, he was scared to tell anyone what had happened. After too many sleepless nights riddled with guilt about whether he could have saved them, he finally decided to talk to the one person he completely trusted in Kanab - Sheriff Marks.

Luckily, or not depending on how he looked at it, the sheriff had seen his share of the inexplicable in and around Kane County and accepted everything Eddie said at face value.

"I have a suggestion," the sheriff had said. "I know you

probably don't want to tell anyone what you just told me, goodness knows there's folks and forces that wouldn't think twice about harnessing what you have for profit or worse, but I think that you were given this gift to help people. I suggest you find a way to do just that."

"How?" Eddie asked.

"I don't know if you're aware, but the town has a hospice centre out on 89. Do you know what a hospice is?"

Eddie shook his head.

"Basically, it's specialised healthcare for people who are close to death. It's also called end-of-life care. They get special treatment for pain and whatever else is needed as they get closer to passing on. One of the biggest problems they have at the centre is being able to give the relatives enough warning to gather bedside and say their goodbyes. Sometimes the patients won't even be aware that their friends and family are there, but the family will know and won't have to suffer the guilt of missing one visit too many, if you get my drift."

"I do," Eddie said, nodding, starting to understand.

"What if after school or chores, you swing by every day and take hold of their hands and see what you feel. If you get that electric feeling, tell the head nurse."

"I guess I could do that."

"I know you can."

As Eddie was about to leave, Marks had held out his hand.

"What's that for?" Eddie had asked.

"For being brave and coming here today to tell me. Most kids won't have done that."

Eddie shook the sheriff's hand.

"In case you're interested, I don't feel the tingle," Eddie advised.

"Glad to hear it," Sheriff Marks said with a smile.

School seemed to drag on for way longer than normal. Eddie would have sworn that there were long periods in math class when the hands of the wall clock stopped moving altogether. It wasn't until art class at the end of the day when time begin to move at a more normal speed. Eddie assumed that was because it was his favourite class, plus he had a little crush on Miss Akins, the substitute teacher who was filling in while Mrs Clarkson was away having yet another baby.

Miss Akins was old, probably in her twenties, but there was something about the way her cheeks dimpled when she smiled that melted Eddie's heart. The fact that on hot days like that day, she'd wear a thin summer dress that fitted her in all the right places didn't hurt either.

After class, Eddie made his way to the new gym for basketball practice. He was a reserve guard and didn't get too much time off the bench during a game, but he still enjoyed every minute of it.

That particular afternoon, the coach was running a two-on-one drill that required the player on defence to prevent the other two players from scoring a basket.

Eddie didn't have a height advantage, so he figured that his best defensive strategy was to use his quickness to get in position to block any shot attempts.

The drill yielded routine results: the expected mix of easy layups and defensive stops, until the final few moments. That's when Eddie mistimed his leap and collided hard with

Bill Wayans, the shooter.

Wayans wasn't just a power forward. He was a power everything. Even at twelve, he was nearly six feet tall and looked more like a football running back. So when Eddie ran smack into him, Wayans hardly budged, sending Eddie careening off him before thumping off the hardwood and coming to rest flat on his back.

"Sorry man," Eddie said looking up at the towering kid.

"No sweat, little man," Wayans said as he offered his hand to help him up.

The moment Eddie grabbed it, he felt the electrical surge pass through his body.

"Everything okay?" Wayans asked, seeing the look of worry on his teammate's face.

"Yeah," Eddie lied. "Just got a little winded there for a moment."

Eddie didn't even bother with a shower. He went straight to the hospice centre to see what the results would be there. He started at the farthest room down the hall and gently knocked.

"Come," a weak voice responded.

Willy Jenkins was ninety-four, blind in one eye and had a grand total of four teeth left in his mouth. Despite all that, he still had some colour in his cheeks and a wry, if vulgar, sense of humour.

"Eddie. I wasn't expecting you so early."

"Just thought I'd swing by on my way home," Eddie replied.

"Why? Got some big plans? Maybe a little saliva swapping with your girlfriend?"

"Don't have a girlfriend at the moment. Just wanted to get home and do some studying."

"You're not one of those idiots who are planning to watch that damn space rock go by are you? Even if you have a big enough telescope, it's just going to be a little blip in the sky."

"No. That's not why. I just have stuff to think about."

"The only thing a boy your age should be thinking about is finding a nice girl so you can start investigating what you both got going on below the belt line."

Eddie was used to Willy's crass comments but that didn't stop him feeling a little uncomfortable every time he produced a new one.

"You here to shake my hand again?" Willy asked. "Strangest damn thing I ever heard of. I mean, it's not as if a handshake if going make any of us any better."

"You never know," Eddie replied. "People say that just by touch, it can bring comfort to certain people."

"I don't think I'm one of those people but, go ahead. Shake away."

Willy held out his emaciated, liver-spotted hand."

Eddie reached over and shook it.

It took Eddie almost an hour to shake all the patients' hands at the centre. As he was walking out the door, the duty nurse called him back.

"What about me?" she asked.

"What about you?"

"Don't I get a handshake like everyone else?"

"Sorry Tina. I didn't think you'd want one," Eddie replied as he shook her hand.

Once back in the parking lot he retrieved his mountain bike and started pedalling home.

Once he reached the junction of 89 and 89a, the rest of the ride home was uphill. It was a tough cycle on a good day, but on that one, it was torture.

Eddie just couldn't get his head into focusing on the pedals and the rough-paved road. His mind was filled with so many confused, abstract thoughts that he could hardly concentrate on much of anything.

It was understandable though.

After shaking a total of eighteen hands so far that day, including, Henry, Wayans, even Tina, he had felt the electric charge pass through him after every single one.

Chapter 3

When he walked through the front door of their adobe style home on Vermillion Road, both his mom and dad were glued to the TV. CNN had a panel of experts discussing the upcoming asteroid that was going pass close to earth. While NASA had formally named it a near-earth object, the Alessi asteroid was going to miss earth by over seven hundred thousand miles. Over twice the distance between the earth and the moon.

Experts were insisting that there was no chance whatsoever of a course change causing the three mile wide lump of rock and metal ore to target their little blue planet.

The most exciting thing about this particular near-earth encounter was that Juniper Logistics' president, Carl Betto, was sending up one of his own rockets so that he could try and land a communications satellite right on top of the asteroid. Considering that Alessi was estimated to be travelling at over forty-eight thousand miles an hour, the odds of success were slim, however, doing the impossible was what Carl Betto was known for.

"Come and watch this with us," his dad called out. "This is going to be historic."

"What? Watching another billionaire crashing a rocket onto a planet. Big whoopee."

Eddie shook his head and walked back to his room, slipping on his headphones to listen to some music in an effort to calm the turmoil in his mind.

As Eddie lay on his bed wondering what could cause that many people to give him the tingling sensation, the doorbell rang. Eddie looked out his window and saw the unmistakable shape and colour of a UPS van. He was about to let someone else answer it but suddenly had a thought. All the people he'd shaken hands with lived in Kanab. The UPS drivers came from St. George or even farther south.

He ran to the door, beating his dad by a few seconds. The brown uniformed delivery man grinned down at him. "Must be something important," he offered.

"Yeah," Eddie replied as he took the box. "Thank you." Eddie held out his hand.

Surprised but amused, the man shook the boy's hand then walked back to his van.

Eddie watched him go as he waited for the electrical tingling to subside before he went back to his room.

What his impromptu experiment told him was that whatever was going to happen wasn't something local. If all the people he'd shaken hands with were going to die, it wasn't just focused on Kanab.

"Mom?" he called out. "Did you get any check-ins today from anywhere interesting?"

"Not today, I'm afraid. The couple in unit 2 are from Flagstaff so that's hardly what you'd call interesting. Mrs Zang checked in yesterday. She's from China and is only here till tomorrow morning. Is that intriguing enough for you?"

Eddie charged out the front door and ran to the back of

their property where they had built two separate apartments in the hope of jumping onto the VRBO rental craze.

As he rounded their triple-wide garage, he saw Mrs Zang sitting outside her unit drinking a cup tea as she sketched the high desert scenery.

Mrs Zang looked up as Eddie approached. She had a round, pretty face framed with jet black hair cut into a bob.

"Hi," Eddie said as he approached.

"You must be the son I've heard so much about," Mrs Zang said in perfect English.

"I guess. I just wanted to come down and welcome you to Kanab." He held his hand out.

Mildly surprised, she shook it.

"Can I get you a cup of tea," she asked.

"Ah … no. Thanks. I got to get going."

Eddie ran back up the hill, terrified at the fact that Mrs Zang had given him the same tingling shock as everyone else that day.

Once inside, his parents insisted that he sit between them on their oversized sofa so he could watch the landing attempt. The lander had so many cameras mounted on it that the video looked more like a well-produced sci-fi movie than a real space mission. The quality and detail of the images were sharp and as clear as anything he'd ever seen.

The lander was approaching the asteroid, somehow matching its extraordinary speed. The mission control spokesman was giving a play-by-play dialogue of exactly what was going on.

The craft was planning to pass in front of the rock then

decelerate just enough so that the forward speed of the asteroid would allow it to slowly catch up to it, resulting in a gentle landing unwittingly powered by the asteroid itself.

The announcer advised that the lander was about to turn in front of the asteroid and begin its slow decrease in speed so that it would be traveling at exactly five miles an hour slower than the giant rock.

As the world watched live, the lander slowly started to turn then suddenly swung violently to the left.

The commentary stopped for almost thirty seconds, after which the man, his hand against his earpiece, continued.

"It appears that a fragment of the asteroid may have separated and struck the lander. They should have it back under control in a matter of seconds," the announcer advised.

As they watched, the lander seemed to stabilize for a moment then began to accelerate. Within seconds, it was clear that it was out of control and was reaching terminal velocity as it heading straight for the asteroid.

The cameras kept working perfectly right up until the lander collided with the giant rock.

There was silence both in the control room and in their living room.

On the TV a huge video screen that had been showing the asteroid trajectory taking it safely past earth began to flash red. The gentle arc of its original path began to bend.

"It appears," the commentator said, "that the asteroid's trajectory is starting to shift. While this may sound alarming, I assure you that we have nothing to fear. We should have the final computation within a few seconds, but rest assured.

It won't come anywhere near us."

Eddie took hold of his parents' hands as they waited for the update. The electrical surge that flowed from them both was strangely comforting. It was important that they be together. Maybe the astrophysicists were still crunching the numbers, but Eddie already knew which way the planet killer was heading.

"Ladies and gentlemen …" the commentator started to say before the screen suddenly went blank. Moments later, the presidential seal filled the screen as a discombobulated voice began to speak. "We are interrupting this program for a special announcement from the President."

LOST WORDS

Chapter 1

Jeff was a terrible writer.

His agent and uncle, Murray Reynolds, had hoped early on that his nephew would eventually start to show some sort of literary promise, but that had been almost twenty years ago. Since then, Jeff had written twelve novels, none of which were ever published. The fact was, they were bad. While not a particularly descriptive term, it fit Jeff's works to a tee. It wasn't a case of the prose not being stirringly inciteful, or the stories themselves lacking in scope. It was that everything about them was mediocre.

Jeff kept writing, knowing that somewhere inside him was a great novel trying to find its way out. But after two decades, he couldn't even get Murray, uncle or not, to call him back. Because of his writing, Jeff had given up a well-paying position on Madison Avenue and had walked away from anything that even closely resembled a career. Instead, he chose short term, low-paying jobs that left him free to spend hours every day in front of his outdated laptop.

It was shortly after finishing the initial draft of his thirteenth manuscript that he felt the weight of his failure as an author descend upon him. He knew deep down that his latest attempt was just was as bad as all the others.

The saddest thing was that he wasn't short on ideas.

Most great writers will tell you that they have to pry the narratives from a subconscious melee of memories and thoughts. Jeff, on the other hand, couldn't stop the ideas from whirring around his head. In fact, there were so many of them vying for attention that he was hardly able to keep up with them.

The problem was that when he tried to put those ideas into words, he just couldn't create the characters or the environments in which they needed to exist.

The melancholy that suddenly consumed him as he finished his latest unexceptional work wasn't only because of the mess he'd made of his life, it was also because it was his birthday. Yet another one that he'd be spending alone.

Jeff decided that he needed to get out of his studio apartment and get some air, hoping a walk would get his blood flowing and inspiration with it. Despite all good intentions, he very quickly found himself at the Longshore Tavern a few blocks from his walk-up apartment. While some businesses in Manhattan's Hell's Kitchen had trendified themselves as the neighbourhood was hit by a slow renewal, his local bar hadn't caught such a bug. Like his home, it was rundown and seedy. Jeff didn't care. As long as he had a roof over his head, a laptop and a place to get cheap drinks, his needs were met.

Despite having frequented the Longshore for close to fifteen years, the bartender never seemed to acknowledge him as a regular. In fact on some nights, he treated Jeff like a complete stranger.

Jeff sat in the darkest corner of the bar and quietly drank himself into a semi-stupor. After all, it was his birthday and even though he didn't have much in the way of expendable wealth, he didn't see the harm in filling the tank all the way up to celebrate the start of his fifty-fifth year.

Stumbling home on West 47th Street, he paused in front of the Cavalry Christian Church. Jeff was hardly what you'd call a man of faith, but for some reason, on that particular night, he felt the need to pray.

He weaved his way to the front door and tried to pull it open. It wouldn't budge. He tried pushing it with the same result. He then saw a posted sign showing the church's opening and closing hours.

"When the hell did that happen?" he slurred, unaware that crime within the city had forced most houses of worship to close at night.

Jeff started to cry. He had so desperately wanted to speak to God and here he was, shut out from even that simple ritual. He decided that he was going to have his conversation with or without being able to enter the building. With tears still streaming down his face, Jeff kneeled on the hard concrete steps, closed his eyes and lowered his head in prayer.

"God, I know that I haven't been much of a believer, but I always knew that you were out there somewhere and would help me if I really needed you. Well, I need you now. I need a favour. I need you to help me write one great novel. I don't care about the money. Before I die, I just want people to know that I really can write. I know it's a lot to ask, and I haven't got anything to offer you in return, but I'm begging you. Please help me."

"You have a lot to offer in return," a voice said.

Jeff opened his eyes and saw a man sitting a few feet away on the same steps. He was dressed in jeans and a hoodie.

"What if I were to promise you that you could write an exceptional novel in exchange for something that you hardly ever use?"

"What's that?" Jeff asked, his words slurred.

"Your soul," the man replied.

Jeff's initial reaction was to laugh. The man's Faustian offer was too absurd. Jeff tried to stand up but the man grabbed his arm. His strength was both unexpected and alarming. His grasp felt like an iron vice.

"This is not a joke," the man said, as he moved closer.

The strange thing was that Jeff still couldn't see the man's face. Sure, it was nighttime, but there were streetlights and the hoodie could only conceal so much. Oddly, the man's eyes were completely visible. They were an astonishing shade of light brown that looked almost golden. Then there were the pupils. They were huge. They took up almost the entire iris.

The other disconcerting thing about the stranger was his breath. It wasn't bad or anything that simple. It was hot. When he spoke, Jeff could feel the heat singeing his hair and eyebrows.

"All I am offering," the man said, "is a simple swap. You agree to give up your soul when you die, and in exchange, I will give you the ability to write the book you've always fantasised about."

Jeff tried to pull away, but the vice-like grip grew even tighter.

"This isn't some sort of trick or a con," the man insisted. "My offer is that I will enable you to write your book, then, once it's finished, I get your soul."

"What if I don't finish?" Jeff asked.

"You will finish. You have my word," the man whispered, sending a new wave of searing heat onto Jeff's face.

Jeff knew that there was no way that he could break free from the crazed lunatic, so he agreed, hoping that would satisfy him and he would find someone else to threaten.

Sure enough, the moment that Jeff accepted the terms, the man rose and walked off into the night.

Jeff returned to his tiny apartment and was about to collapse onto his sagging bed when he came up with the most amazing opening for his book. He sat in front of his ancient laptop and began writing.

Douglas looked down at the desert floor as it spread out before him. From his position, hundreds of feet up on the rust-coloured cliff, the land looked barren and lifeless. He of course knew that wasn't the case at all. The parched surface was teaming with life, all struggling against the blazing heat and arid conditions, but it was still, life.

In the far distance, Douglas could see glimmers of civilisation. Light reflected off hidden windows, a thin swirl of woodsmoke rose into the sky and just beyond was the vague outline of a water tower, tucked into the red rocks behind the town.

He'd made it back to Champagne, Arizona.

Jeff had no idea where the words were coming from, but didn't care. He was writing at a level he never thought was possible.

Within a month, Jeff had written over twenty thousand words. Good words. Words that could change everyone's opinion about his talent as a writer. At least that was his belief. The problem was going to be how to get someone else to read what he was writing. It took six tries before Murray called him back and after some serious grovelling, his agent finally agreed to read the first two chapters.

Jeff's phone rang less than a week later. Murray wanted to read more.

Jeff sent him the balance of what he'd written so far and one week later, he was sitting across from Murray in his midtown office.

"I don't know what to say, Jeff," Murray said. "This is good. I'm talking exceptionally good. Is this really your writing? I hate to ask, but, it's nothing like anything of yours that I've ever read."

"I know," Jeff replied. "If I can keep it up, do you think it's something that you might get a publisher to look at?"

"I already sent your initial pages to the big publishers. All of them have shown a definite interest."

"Seriously?" Jeff was shocked.

"Jeff, this is without question some of the best writing I've ever read in my life. If you can keep the narrative and this quality of writing through to the end, you will have a best seller."

Jeff often thought of that night when he encountered the hooded man. Even though his new-found talent came soon after that meeting, he refused to accept that the two events were related in any way.

When thoughts of the hooded man surfaced in his head, Jeff would remind himself that running across crazy people on the streets of New York was not that unusual. Finding one that offered you talent in exchange for your soul was probably a little more rare, but still not unheard of.

Jeff made it a point not to hark back to the church steps. After all, looking for any plausibility in something like that was almost certainly the first step on a road to some sort of mental deterioration. One minute you believe what the street people are saying, the next, you're wearing a tinfoil hat and prophesising the end of the world because of the chemicals found in chicken nuggets.

Chapter 2

Jeff wrote every day. If anything, his wordsmithing and storytelling were actually improving. In a show of faith, Murray bought him a brand new laptop and set him up with high-speed internet access. The only condition was that he wanted Jeff to email each day's pages the moment he finished writing them.

Though Murray insisted that he was just verifying the quality of Jeff's output, the fact was, he couldn't wait for the next few pages to see where the writer was going to transport him to next.

As Murray stood waiting at his monitor as pages 101 through 107 populated the screen. He began reading the moment that the first page was fully uploaded.

Helen stared at him as if seeing him for the first time. Ever since he'd returned to Champagne, she'd noticed the change. Douglas had been a fresh-faced teen when he left soon after the twin towers fell. He'd signed up to fight against people he'd only heard about from TV or movies. He told anyone who asked that any man that walked around wearing a dress and couldn't be bothered to shave, wasn't very likely to be much of a fighter.

The man that now stood before her had found that Afghanis were vicious fighters. They had none of the

114

dazzling munitions that Uncle Sam provided, at least not recently, but that didn't stop them from killing half his platoon the first week he was in country.

On the day that Douglas left for what was to be his third tour of duty, Helen had given herself to him. If wasn't as if they hadn't been dating for a while, she just had this dumb idea about not wanting him to return to war still a virgin. She hadn't expected any particular reciprocity from him, but had been shocked when she found that he had decided not to return to see her on his leaves. Instead, he stayed on a base in Northern Virginia and pretty much kept to himself.

There'd only been one phone call from him early on in his deployment. He explained that he couldn't come home until it was all over. Until he knew that he wouldn't be going back to the fighting. He was scared that if he spent time in his hometown, especially with the girl he loved more than life itself, he'd remember all the things he missed so very much and might not find the courage needed to go back to the fighting.

Murray read all seven pages and smiled to himself. Jeff wasn't just writing a book, he was creating an American saga. He poured himself a small scotch and settled himself into his favourite chair so he could read the pages slowly, savouring every word.

Three months later, Jeff could sense that he'd crested the bulk of the manuscript and had started on the downward slope. He hoped he was right. Not knowing what he was going to write each day was surprisingly stressful. He would agonise all night, terrified that no words would be forthcoming the following morning. Yet they did. Day after day after day the words came and the story unfolded.

David held her tighter than either of them thought possible. It was getting dark which meant that the sheriff would be coming back from...

Jeff stopped typing and stared at the words on the page.

"Who the hell is David?" he laughed.

Jeff deleted David and replaced it with Douglas then continued typing, thinking nothing of the minor character error. He wrote eight pages that day and was pleased with the result. He sent them to Murray then waited for the daily phone call telling him that they were great as usual.

The call didn't come as fast as it usually did. Jeff assumed that his agent was taking his time reading the pages.

The fact was that Murray was reading them over and over again, but not because of the story. It was the errors that were keeping his eyes rivetted to the pages. The first chapter alone was enough to have sent an icy chill all the way up from the base of his spine. The pages that he was seeing looked nothing like what Jeff believed he had typed.

Douglas held hur tighter than eether of them thoght possible. It was getting dark which meant that the sherf would be on his woy buck from the site of the crash. If what they beared was true, and Rachel really was deed, all of their blanning and subtrafuge would have been for mothing. With the matriarch of the family bone, old wounds would reolen and the bars between the fanchers would soon tart agin. There qas only on way that could be stopped before it even started.

gelen would have to assume thefole she was birn to, an necome the leader of the Taylor damily.

116

Murray was used to seeing early pages from writers that had way more mistakes than Jeff's. The concern was that the other writers always made mistakes. Jeff never did. Even in his earlier writing, the content may have been sub-par, but the spelling and grammar was always perfect.

Murray finally called Jeff and told him that he would be right over.

Jeff assumed that it was to offer him some praise in person for the last few pages. He could tell the moment he opened the door that Murray was not there to gush. He had Jeff sit at his laptop and copy a paragraph from a book written by another of his clients.

Murray stood behind him and watched as Jeff typed while looking at the unfamiliar text.

If anything, there were even more errors than in the pages Jeff had sent earlier that same evening. Murray made an appointment for Jeff to meet with his personal doctor. He hoped that the explanation ended up being something simple like eye strain or exhaustion, after all, Jeff had been driving himself pretty hard.

The doctor examined Jeff and, after giving him a series of cognitive tests, sent him for a brain scan. The results were not conclusive. He decided to have Jeff rescanned one week later. That time there was no doubt.

Jeff appeared to have early onset Alzheimer's. For a man in his mid-fifties, Jeff was extremely unlucky to have been hit with the disease. What worried the doctor most was how fast the illness appeared to be manifesting in the patient. Within one week, the brain scan went from looking normal to there being a visible reduction in the size of Jeff's temporal and parietal lobes.

The doctor was able to enrol Jeff in an experimental treatment from the Rose Pharmaceutical Company but was concerned that in Jeff's case, too much damage had already been done.

When the doctor first told him about his diagnosis, Jeff shook his head and told him that the tests were wrong. He felt fine and the writing issue was just because of eye strain. But as the weeks went by, Jeff started noticing other problems. He began forgetting things like his laptop password and even Murray's phone number.

It wasn't until he was walking home from the local supermarket and for a moment didn't recognise his surroundings that he started to worry.

Each night, Jeff still emailed his pages to Murray and was unaware of how much work his agent had to do to make them legible. Murray had hired an intern whose sole job was to transcribe Jeff's writings at the end of each week. At first, the intern had found the task ludicrously easy, especially for someone with a master's degree in creative writing, but as the weeks wore on, the text became harder and harder to de-code.

A month later, Jeff was no longer living in his studio as by that point his condition required continuous supervision. Murray had found a five star residential treatment facility only twenty minutes outside Manhattan. He had his own room and most importantly, a desk and his laptop so he could continue writing.

Jeff spent at least five hours a day writing, determined to

finish the book while he could still manage to think at all.

Finally it became so difficult to decipher his writing that Angela felt she had to show Murray an example of what Jeff was sending:

Harshnt spoht ig a lod n clwr vobe. E wnred o nsre ht eryon tgr cold ho rim clrky. Te ntnall ws pckt as jut abut evy sngl resint of Cmpagn wntd te her fr hemsves wht e ad yo sy.

Murray couldn't bear to read any more. He spent the next hour persuading Angela to try a completely new tactic in the battle to understand Jeff's deteriorating words. Though far below her skill level, she agreed to sit with Jeff every day, transcribing his spoken words into legible print.

Soon, even that became an arduous task. Jeff would forget what he was saying halfway through paragraphs. Angela had to literally coax the words out of him, one sentence at a time.

By the end of her second week with Jeff at the facility, it was taking longer and longer to fill each page. The frustrating thing was that the story was getting close to the end. At one point, she even wondered if she could write the final words herself. Before she had to resort to something so unethical, a minor miracle took place.

Angela arrived at her usual time and as she made her way to Jeff's room, she was terrified in case his condition had deteriorated overnight. What she saw when she opened the door made her gasp.

Jeff had showered, shaved and was wearing jeans and a clean t-shirt. He looked almost normal, were it not for the slight facial tick he'd developed a few weeks earlier. He hadn't waited for her to arrive and had been typing.

"Sorry to have started without you," he said, his voice raspy from overusing it the last few days. "I feel better today."

"So I see," Angela replied as she stood looking over his shoulder.

There were errors, dozens of them, but the work was legible. It was as if he gone back to how he'd been a full month earlier. Angela spent the day alongside him as he emailed one page at a time to her so she could do the correcting on-site.

The next morning, for the first time in ages, she wasn't dreading spending the day with Jeff. She actually stopped by a Starbucks on the way and bought a couple of lattes and carrot cake.

"I thought you'd like a little treat today," she said as she stepped into his room.

She almost dropped the coffees. Jeff wasn't sitting at the desk. He was lying flat on his bed with his eyes staring, unblinking up at the ceiling. A little dribble of saliva had made it as far as his chin.

A nurse suddenly entered the room.

"I wanted to warn you before you saw him," she stated, breathless. "He's taken a turn."

"When did this happen?"

"About an hour ago. He was working at the computer then suddenly stopped. I was actually in the room, and thought I heard him say something."

"What do you think he said?" Angela asked.

"I can't be certain because his speech was deteriorating but if I had to guess, I think he said, 'fuck you, Satan.'"

Angela walked over to Jeff's laptop and opened it. It booted up almost immediately and opened a document. The last page sent a shiver throughout her body as her eyes welled up with tears.

It simply read: THE ...

Almost one year later to the day, Murray stood outside the Strand Bookstore on Broadway and smiled at the window display. *Remembering the Future* by Jeff Whitehead filled two entire windows. He stood back and took a picture so he could show Jeff that he'd finally gotten his wish. Everyone now knew that he could write.

As he put his phone back in his jacket pocket, a wave of sadness swept over him like a January fog. Jeff had died only a few hours after Angela had found him. Maybe out of kinship, or more likely an unconscious sense of guilt at having ignored Jeff for so long, Murray stopped by the graveyard across the river in Jersey and read the latest reviews or the status of the battle over the movie rights.

The one thing that kept nagging at him was that Jeff had promised that, despite the Alzheimer's, he would complete the manuscript before he died or his brain ceased to function altogether.

The thing was, legally, Jeff never finished the book, at least not according to accepted literary norms. By not finishing with the wording 'THE END', the manuscript was incomplete. Murray himself had covertly added the last word, in effect being the person to actually finish the saga.

Obviously the world still knew that Jeff was the author of the bestseller, but something about his having left the one word out still troubled him.

Murray turned away from the window display and bumped into a man in a black hoody.

"Sorry," Murray mumbled.

"Don't be," the man said.

Murray looked towards the man and was surprised that he couldn't see his face, only his bright golden eyes and dilated pupils. The other weird thing was that Murray was pretty sure that he could feel the man's breath and it was hot. Not just hot. It felt as if he was standing too close to an open fire.

Murray started to turn away but the man reached out and grabbed his arm, except it didn't feel like any human grip. It was just like the pressure from a blood pressure cuff except it grew tighter and tighter.

"We have things to discuss," the man said.

"What things?" Murray asked, his voice strained by the pain in his arm.

"Soulful things," the man whispered.

LABOUR SHORTAGE

Chapter 1

Melissa Hart hated her job. After a total of four years getting her bachelor's and then master's in agriculture, she had hoped to land herself a high paying position at a national think tank that focussed on the nation's food supply and its logistics counterpart.

Instead, Mel had ended up as an assistant manager carrying out nationwide productivity analysis for the new Minister of State at the Department for Environment, Food and Rural Affairs. She basically spent her days in a cramped cubicle in Whitehall crunching data from across England.

What made the job all the more frustrating was that Mel had spent a year flirting and sucking up to the previous Minister who had promised that he would get her into a manager's slot within the ministerial support team by the start of the year.

Then the political world imploded.

Thanks to the Prime Minister being charged with lewd conduct and, of all things, pandering, he was forced to resign. In a show of 'understanding the needs of the public', the new PM chose to replace almost every cabinet minister with fresh and untarnished allies.

Mel's new boss was almost certain to be immune to Mel's 'sycophantic' plan for promotion as Sheila Winters, the MP for Hounslow South, was immune to any form of brown-nosing. Mel was therefore faced with only two options, neither of which were particularly appealing. Focusing on her work and making a real go of it, or trying to find something else. Considering the lean pickings that were available in the job market, she was forced to stay where she was. It didn't matter that the pay was reasonably good or that, if she kept her head down, the position was relatively secure. Staring at a computer screen filled with data about everything from manure sampling versus crop output to courgette length in relation to location and rain cycles, was enough to fry her brain.

The latest focus of the department was on the catastrophic shortage of seasonal farm workers. Mel still couldn't fathom how those who were supposed to be running the country hadn't for one second considered what would happen if all the EU temp labourers who, on an annual basis, helped ensure that English crops were harvested, were suddenly not permitted entry or employment in the UK because of Brexit.

Millions of acres of produce were literally dying on the vine because of a lack of pickers. And in addition to that, summer temperatures were reaching African proportions, which meant that a fast harvesting was essential to avoid the crops succumbing to the brutally hot and dry weather.

Yet the country no longer had enough pickers.

What really shocked Mel was that, instead of the government finding an immediate solution, they chose instead to have people like Mel evaluating data that, no matter how it could be spun, always came up with the same information.

No pickers. No picking.

Mel's latest data dump was focused on harvesting productivity throughout the UK. Some brainiac had created a data grid dividing the entire country into neat little two acre squares. Mel and the other 'analysts' had to convert harvest data from every farm and field in the country in such a way as to be able to click on any two-acre square and see exactly what was produced, how much of that was successfully harvested and how long the process took.

Mel ran her hand through her purple-streaked hair as she manually entered each crop's harvesting stats into the new algorithm. She'd been doing that for six weeks and already knew that all her efforts were going to show exactly the same shortfall. Eighteen percent of UK crops were dying before they could be harvested. It didn't matter which two acre grid she added to the mix, the overall numbers hardly varied one little bit.

After entering data from a cooperative farming community in Worcestershire , the eighteen hundred and fifty-three grids that made up their co-op began flashing green. Mel had never seen that happen before and was momentarily stunned.

She brought up the raw data she'd just entered and after a few minutes crunching the numbers, found the anomaly that had been flagged by the software.

For the past six years, the current tracking period, the farming community of West Witching had managed to harvest their entire combined apple crop without any evidence of loss or delay.

At first Mel decided that the area must simply have a higher demographic of young adults who were able to come together and pick the fruit. On a hunch, Mel checked the age demographic in and around the small village and was surprised to see that the median age of the entire area was sixty two.

Mel walked over to her manager's office to tell him what she'd found, but as usual, Brett Grant was far more interested in tossing around rude (and more recently, illegal) sexual innuendos about how she looked and how much 'fun' they could have together if she'd only go out for a drink with him.

When she finally managed to get him to focus on the data she had brought for him to see, Brett seemed not the least bit interested and instead started telling her about this great new pub just across Westminster Bridge.

"We were supposed to report any data anomalies that was found by the software," Mel said, hoping that her manager would for once look at her eyes instead of her breasts.

"Come on, love. We all know that this whole thing's a load of bollocks. So you managed to find a tiny area that's actually productive. So what. Why don't do we grab a few pints after work and I'll show you some real productivity."

"That doesn't even make sense," Mel shot back without thinking.

"I'll tell you what doesn't make sense," Brett said with a forced smile. "You being so damned frigid. Look at you. I bet under all that makeup and hair dye, you'd actually be almost attractive."

Mel took a deep breath as she talked herself out of telling Brett what she really thought about him. Especially as she would almost certainly be the one who ended up in HR being reprimanded for aggressive workplace behaviour.

"What do you want me to do with this data, then?" Mel asked, trying to keep the anger from her voice.

"I don't bloody care. If you think it's that important, why not nip up to this pinprick of productivity and check it out."

"It's in Worcestershire," Mel reminded him.

"Better still. You can get a hotel for the night and make a mini break out of it," Brett replied. "I'll sign off on the expenses so long as it's not the Ritz."

"You want me to visit the farm?"

"Someone's got to check it out and I'm certainly not going to bloody Worcestershire. If I want sauce, I can find it much closer to home, if you get my drift."

Mel turned and started to walk away not wishing to have anything more to go with her predatory manager.

"Don't forget to text me the hotel name and number, just in case I decide you're worth a long drive."

Chapter 2

Mel left work at lunch time and rented a ZipCar less than a hundred metres from her Lambeth flat. Once out of London, the drive to West Witching took two and a half hours including a brief stop at a service area so she could buy herself a sandwich for the drive.

Following the instructions from her Waze app, she turned off the M5 just past Worcester and soon found herself on a single lane road bordered by six foot high hedgerows. After five miles of seeing no evidence of civilisation, a small hand-made sign with the words West Witching pointed down a rutted road off to the right.

Mel started to worry when the road began narrowing to the point that the vegetation was starting to scratch against the sides of her rental. She was looking for somewhere to turn around when the road emerged into a village green that was surrounded by apple trees as far as she could see.

West Witching consisted of a pub (where she was spending the night), a neat row of white-washed terraced houses, a small general store, and a Norman church. Mel tried to find some beauty in the setting, but there was something about the surrounding apple trees that made the place claustrophobic.

Mel pulled up in front of the Iron Cauldron free house and

once out of the rented Ford, took a moment to look at the pub. When she'd booked her room online, the minimal blurb simply mentioned its storied history, but gave no indication of how old it was or what made its history worthy of said stories. Judging by the ancient, blackened timbers and the white surrounding mortar, Mel assumed it could be Elizabethan, though something made her think it might just be older than even that.

Once inside, Mel felt as if she had been carried back in time. The pub was low ceilinged with a worn stone floor. The walls were painted a dark green and the furnishings were made of heavy woods and dark red leather.

The main room was about four metres square with a rough-hewn wooden bar at one end. The windows were small and heavily leaded allowing little light to reach far enough inside to make much of a difference.

There were no customers, however Mel made note that it was only just past three-thirty and that if the village really was as productive as the data had led her to believe, everyone was probably out picking at that very moment.

"Can I help you?" a voice said from somewhere behind the bar.

"I booked a room for tonight, the name's Melissa Hart."

An older man appeared from the shadows and stepped out from behind the bar. He was tall enough that he had to stoop under the low ceiling and judging by his lean physique and ruddy complexion, Mel assumed he spent a lot of time in the orchards.

"I assumed that might have been the case, Ms Hart," the man said. "We don't get that many visitors out here."

"That's a shame," Mel said, while wondering what possible reason anyone would have to visit such a lonely place. "It's such a pretty spot."

The man simply shrugged. "Your room is ready. There's nothing hot in the kitchen as you've missed lunch, but I could put together some cheese and bread if you like."

"I'm fine, thank you. I have an appointment to meet with Peter Maxton at the cooperative farm building."

"You're lucky that we've been rain free for a few days, otherwise the trek can be a bit muddy."

"Can't I drive there?"

"Not easily. You'd have to know the roads and farm tracks like the back of your hand. It's much easier to just cut through a couple of orchards. There's even colour-coded pathways that start from the village green out front. There's painted rocks along the way, so all you have to do is to stay on the blue path then turn left onto the red one and you'll reach the shed in about ten minutes."

"Shed?" Mel said, surprised.

"We call it that, but it's a tad bigger than your average garden model."

After dumping her wheelie bag in her room and using the shared toilet, Mel followed the publican as he led her across the green to a narrow pathway that led between the apple trees, their branches laden with ripe fruit.

"Just stick to the paths and you'll be fine. At least in the daylight hours."

"What happens if for some reason I get lost?" Mel asked, only half kidding.

"It's harvest time. We'll find you soon enough and you'll

certainly have enough to eat while you wait - that's if you like apples."

Mel smiled and was about to start down the path when a thought struck her.

"I don't see anyone out harvesting at the moment. Isn't that a little unusual?"

"They harvest from east to west so you wouldn't see or hear much from here. Besides, the cooperative only picks at night."

Mel nodded as if that made any sense then stepped between two sizeable trees and soon found herself in near darkness because of the canopy of foliage. As she walked farther into the orchard she noticed that the only sound was that of her own footfalls.

It only took about eight minutes to reach the junction with the red path, but to Mel, it had felt like an eternity. The orchard was giving her a serious case of the creeps, not just because of the silence and gloom, but because of the trees themselves.

She'd been in apple orchards before but had never seen trees of the size or age of those that surrounded her. Mel was sure that she'd read somewhere that the older an apple tree became the less fruit it produced. According to the data, that was not the case in West Witching. Judging by their size and the gnarling of their branches, Mel assumed the trees must have been ancient.

Maybe too ancient.

Mel kept flashing back to when her parents had taken her to the maze at Hampton Court. The memory was still vividly fresh, maybe because two days later they were killed in a head on collision on the M4 after a drunk driver managed to end up going the wrong way on the off-ramp at Junction Nine. His white van was hardly damaged and he received only a few cuts and bruises. Her parents' classic Mini, however, was completely obliterated.

Mel could remember how excited she was about getting to go inside the famed maze, but once they got there, low, charcoal-grey clouds descended to what seemed like only a few feet above the hedge walls. With the foliage rising high above her on all sides and almost all light being cut off by the weather, she soon felt the walls closing in as her claustrophobia kicked in.

Mel was having the same sensation in the orchard. As she started down the red path, she had to control her breathing and prayed that the community shed wasn't much farther ahead.

Despite the calm-inducing breathing exercises and her rational certainty that nothing untoward was going on, Mel became convinced that the trees were somehow closing in behind her, cutting off any possible exit route.

Mel started running. Even though she knew it was impossible, she became convinced that at any moment, the trees ahead of her would uproot and block the path.

Less than a minute later, Mel exploded out of the orchard only a few metres from the co-op shed. Over a dozen locals stopped their unloading of various barrows and stared open mouthed at the young woman with funny coloured hair as she stood gasping for breath while trying to wipe beads of perspiration from her face and neck.

"Hello," Mel gasped. "I'm here from the ministry."

Chapter 3

Mel was led to the shed (which was in fact a large, aluminium-sided building the size of a football pitch). In it, a dozen more villagers were sorting and packing apples that she assumed had been picked the previous night.

One of them was Peter Maxton. At over two hundred and fifty pounds and topped with flaming red hair, he looked formidable. As he approached Mel, she realized that close up, he was much older than he'd appeared at first glance. Mel tried to hide her amusement, when the thought hit her of just how much his face looked a little like a shrivelled up apple.

"So," Peter said as he shook her hand, "our humble little co-op has come to the attention of Whitehall, has it? Well you've caught us red-handed."

Mel gave him a confused look. "I'm not sure..."

"Surely for the government to send someone all the way out here, you must believe that we've been doing something bad."

"Actually, I'm here because your cooperative seems to be doing something right and we want to learn how and why," Mel explained.

Peter studied her for a moment before speaking.

"What exactly are we accused of doing right?"

"You seem to be the only large scale grower who has managed to consistently bring your harvest in on time and without spoilage during this recent labour shortage."

"That's a sad state of affairs when doing something right brings us to the attention of the ministry."

"Normally it wouldn't," Mel explained. "But since Brexit and then covid, there's been a general shortage of pickers which as I'm sure you know has had a negative impact of the entire industry."

"Not here it hasn't, and I'm afraid you've wasted a trip. There's no great secret to how things get done here. We all simply give as much of ourselves as we can and get the bloody job done. It's how this community has survived for well over four hundred years."

"I had no idea the cooperative has been going for that long."

"It's not always been called a co-op, but it's has always been a going concern owned and operated by the villagers."

"That's impressive," Mel said. "Obviously I have to go back and tell the ministry something. Would it be possible for me to observe the picking?"

Peter gave her his warmest smile and answered, "No. I'm afraid that's completely out of the question. You see, one of our longest lasting traditions is that we only harvest the apples at night."

"I don't mind coming back at night."

"I'm afraid that we don't allow observers during the night picking. It's too distracting and upsets the synchronicity between the pickers and the trees."

"The ... what?" Mel thought she'd misheard him.

"That's what we call it anyway. Unlike most industrial apple orchards where the trees are shaken by machinery to loosen the fruit, we do everything by hand, and believe it or not, we feel that the trees prefer that and produce sweeter apples."

"Exactly how many pickers do you have?" Mel asked, deciding not to comment on Peter's new-age bollocks.

"I'll tell you what. Why don't you meet me in the pub bar at eight o'clock and I'll introduce you to the picking crew before they start work."

"Is the pub big enough for them all?"

"They'll fit. Don't worry about that," Peter replied, amused.

After spending the next hour talking to the sorters and packers, Mel made her way back through the orchards. The sun was lower in the sky and even less light managed to reach under the canopy. Within minutes of starting down the red path, Mel again felt the same sense of claustrophobia descend upon her.

Though she knew that she was alone (she looked back every few metres to check), Mel still felt the unease she'd experience earlier. Finally, she stepped out of the darkness and into the last vestiges of light as the sun dipped below the horizon.

Mel returned to her room and typed up her notes. She felt embarrassed at how little she'd learned from the locals. There was nothing that could be used to alleviate the national labour shortage. The fact that they worked hard, kept a positive attitude and shared a mutual sense of responsibility for the harvest was noble, but hardly a process that could be suggested as a solution to the current problem.

After FaceTiming briefly with her sister, who insisted on telling her every single thing she'd done that day, Mel went downstairs to check out the dining room.

It turned out there wasn't a dining room. Instead, four of the tables in the bar were reserved for dining guests, though Mel seemed to be the only one.

There was no menu as the only meal was whatever the publican prepared that day. Thankfully, the current offering was chicken pot pie, one of her favourites. The dish came with chunky chips and mushy peas and Mel washed it all down with a local cider.

By the time she'd finished a ludicrously large slice of apple pie with clotted cream, it was eight o'clock. She looked over as the pub door opened expecting to see a veritable mass of humanity squeeze inside. Instead, Patrick held the door open as nine middle aged locals entered.

Mel stood and was introduced to each of them before they sat around a large table by one of the rooms leaded, bay windows.

She asked when the other pickers would be joining them.

"This is everybody," Patrick replied, smiling.

"Nine of you do all the picking?" Mel asked, trying not to sound too dubious.

"Of course not," one of the men responded.

Mel felt some relief.

"Only eight of us do the picking. Jane over there, she does the coordinating."

After half an hour, Mel had asked them just about anything she could think of to garner some sort of earthshattering revelation as to how so few of them were able to harvest what, at any other orchard, would have taken scores of labourers to complete.

Their unified answer was that they simply respected the trees and worked with an abundance of passion and patience.

Again, not much to report back to the ministry. Mel knew that telling the government that the solution to productive farming in the UK was simply being respectful and passionate about their work was not something that she planned to do. Her choice was to either go back to London and say that they just worked extraordinary hours or keep looking for the missing piece of the puzzle.

Mel decided that the latter was the only real option. As she sat in her room trying to formulate some way to get more information from the farmers, her phone began buzzing on the nightstand.

It was Brett.

"What do you want?" Mel asked. "I was about to go to sleep."

"How's it going out there in the wilds of Worcestershire?"

"Fine. I should have all the data by midday tomorrow," she lied.

"I checked out the village. There is only one hotel, or at least somewhere with rooms. It's some crappy looking pub called the Iron Cauldron. I assume you are staying there?"

Mel didn't want to answer her boss, but knew that she couldn't just ignore the question. "Not much choice."

"I haven't decided yet f I'm going to stop by, so keep one eye open," he said laughing.

"I wish you would stop being so disrespectful to me," Mel said.

"Don't start that nonsense again," Brett shot back. "You're lucky you got to keep your job after the last time you got your knickers in a twist and spoke to HR about me. Didn't you learn anything? Plebs like you are completely expendable. Besides, I saw the way you came on to the last minister, so it's bloody obvious how far you will go for job security and advancement. Maybe the time has come for you to give me the same consideration."

"I'll see you tomorrow afternoon," Mel replied, subdued.

"Don't sound so sad," Brett whispered. "You may just see me in a couple of hours."

Mel disconnected the call and felt anger welling up inside. She was relatively certain that Brett would not drive all the way to Worcestershire, but a tiny voice within her head kept asking, *What if he does?*

She buried her face in one of the bed pillows and screamed until her head hurt.

Chapter 4

While lying flat on her back staring up at the Artex ceiling, Mel realised how she could get more information about the harvesting operation. Despite being told that she couldn't disturb the pickers at work, Peter never said she couldn't sneak a peek at them from a distance.

Mel saw that it was just past ten, so she knew the workers would be picking at the far end of the orchard. She donned her dark windbreaker, grabbed her iPhone and tiptoed down the pub's rickety staircase.

Mel was a little concerned about being able to find the current location of the pickers, but as soon as she stepped outside and crossed the green, she could see a dome of illumination coming from the direction that the blue path seemed to be heading.

Mel once again stepped from the safety of the village green into the oppressively dark orchard. She immediately felt her claustrophobia return even after switching her phone's torch function to full.

Though she knew it was just her imagination, Mel couldn't help but feel that the deeper she went inside the orchard, the closer the apple trees were to each other. She kept pointing her phone light off to the side, convinced that the trees had somehow joined together and created an impassable barrier. The problem was that the phone light didn't reach far enough into the pervasive gloom to reassure her that none of trees had actually moved.

By the time she reached the turning for the red path, Mel was again using calming breathing rhythms to keep her growing panic at bay.

She was sorely tempted to take the red path or even return to the village rather than venture still farther into the vast orchard network. Just as her she was about to give up the chance to witness, albeit secretly, the picking process, Mel had a mental image of Brett's reaction to her final uninspired report.

Mel stood at the path junction and for a full minute closed her eyes and willed herself to continue on.

"Get a grip," she whispered to herself.

Almost immediately, the trees nearest her started to rustle.

Mel broke into a run, but through an astonishing force of willpower, stayed on the blue path.

After a further fifteen minutes, Mel began seeing the vaguest glimmer of illumination filtering through the trees. Within a few minutes there was enough ambient light for her to turn off her phone torch.

Wanting to ensure that she wasn't spotted, Mel left the path and skirted what she believed was the picking area. She kept to the shadows and moved slowly, stopping at each tree to gauge her position in relation to the workers.

Mel suddenly heard voices. She wasn't close enough to make out what was being said, but she knew she had to be nearly there.

She crept a few trees closer and could finally see the pickers less than a hundred feet ahead. Mel moved behind the nearest tree and leant against its trunk.

There was something about the feel of the tree that wasn't right. Mel reached out her hand and lay her palm against the trunk.

She gasped.

The tree was warm. Not only that, but she was almost certain that she had felt a steady, throbbing from deep within the trunk before pulling her hand away.

Mel knew it was impossible, but the steady, even rhythm from within the tree felt like a beating heart.

The need for confirmation somehow outweighed the terror that was rising withing her. Mel placed both palms on the side of the tree and closed her eyes.

She felt the same throbbing and if anything, the trunk was even warmer.

Mel opened her eyes and started at the tree in wonder.

"What in God's name are you?" Mel whispered.

"Nothing to do with god," a voice answered just inches from her ear.

Mel spun around and saw that Peter was smiling down at her, and that the workers were staring open-mouthed only a few metres away.

"I told you that visitors were not permitted to witness the harvest," Peter said.

"I'm sorry. I had to know why your co-op hasn't been affected in any way by the labour shortage."

"Why is that worth risking your life?"

"I'm hardly doing anything that dangerous," Mel shot

back. "If I can't go back to the ministry with some sort of answer, I may as well give up any hope of ever getting promoted."

Peter studied her for a moment then sighed.

"For some reason, the trees appear to have accepted you. That is extraordinarily rare. You must have a good heart, that's all I can say."

"They're trees," Mel said, shaking her head. "What exactly do you think they can do to hurt me?"

"I think perhaps that the easiest way to answer that is to let you watch the harvest process."

Mel felt as if a lead weight had been removed from her shoulders.

"Thank you. I'll try my best not to get in the way."

Peter laughed as he led her towards that night's picking zone.

Chapter 5

Mel had expected to see ladders, picking aprons and all the other paraphernalia that went with large scale apple harvesting. Instead, there were a dozen or so wooden, horse-drawn carts lined up between the trees, and a folding chair had been placed every ten metres or so, facing away from the vehicles. Next to the carts, and laid carefully between the trees, were large green tarps. As she watched, the pickers returned to their assigned seats and bowed their heads.

Mel had assumed that the bright light that she'd seen from as far away as the village green had to have been coming from powerful flood lights of some sort. Instead, the light was coming from three steel barrels spaced evenly next to the carts.

Fire was rising from within the barrels, but instead of the normal yellowy-orange, the flames were blue-white and gave off an extraordinary bright light.

Mel was about to ask what exactly they were burning when Peter helped her up into one of the carts to give her a better view and then stood beside her. She opened her mouth to say something but Peter shook his head sternly and held a finger to his lips, silencing her.

Mel, unable to work out why he was trying to make the

simple act of picking into something mysterious, shrugged her shoulders and looked down the row of seated villagers.

Almost in unison, they all suddenly raised their heads and held their arms out towards the trees. Even from Mel's oblique angle, she could see that the villager's eyes had changed. They all appeared to have taken on a silvery hue while emitting an eerie glow.

She sensed movement all around her. It took a moment for her mind to comprehend what she was seeing. The apple trees were all slowly bending downwards, lowering their fruit-laden branches to the ground. The sound of their contorting trunks and branches filled the air. Once their gnarled trunks were almost perpendicular to the loamy soil, the trees went momentarily still.

Mel felt a scream rising in her throat. Peter, sensing her fear, took her hand gently in his and squeezed it to comfort her.

Just as she thought that the bizarre theatre had finished, the villagers, while still seated on their folding chairs, began to sway from side to side as they vigorously shook their outstretched arms.

Mel watched transfixed as the trees began to quiver then shake as the branches brushed the ground with every motion. Within seconds apples began rolling down from the orchard to the awaiting carts.

The harvesting continued for almost ten minutes at which point the branches suddenly stilled. It wasn't until the villagers raised their hands above their heads that the trees slowly straightened back up and sat unmoving and silent.

The villagers, together with Peter, picked up long

wooden-pronged rakes and began to carefully move the apples onto the tarps. Within half an hour, the tarps were covered with fruit and the pickers lifted each one, one at a time, and gently tipped the apples into a waiting cart.

"You can join us if you want," Peter called to Mel.

Though still shocked at what she'd seen, Mel couldn't help but notice the expression of joy on all the workers' faces.

Mel stepped down from the cart and was handed a rake. She watched how the villagers were rolling the fruit from the top with gentle movements and followed suit.

"So, what do you think?" Peter asked as he stepped alongside her.

"To be honest, I have no idea what to think. This is all completely impossible. You do know that, don't you?"

"All I know is that this is how the cooperative families here have always harvested."

"But how..." Mel began, then a thought hit her. "West Witching," she whispered to herself as the penny dropped.

Peter smiled. "This has been a witching community for almost five hundred years."

"So the villagers were controlling the trees?"

"Yes and no. The trees will only ever do what they want to do. We are simply able to coordinate their actions."

Mel paused her raking as she tried to find the right words for her next question.

"Do they do anything else?"

"Yes," Peter replied as he stopped raking and turned to face her. "They protect us. When every attempt was made to eradicate all witches, a small group began to have visions that led them to these orchards. While the others of our kind were being slaughtered throughout the land, our families stayed hidden and protected right here."

"I don't wish to sound thick but how exactly can an apple tree protect anyone? Throw fruit?"

"Trust me, you don't want to know. Suffice it to say, they can present a formidable barrier if needs be, which brings up an interesting question. How did you manage to walk through the orchard at night?"

Mel gave him a confused look. "The same way I walked through during the day, why?"

"The trees are particularly vigilant when the sun goes down. You should not have made it through to us unscathed. You are extraordinarily lucky."

Peter had a thought.

"Please don't be offended by this question, but is there any history of you having had a relative, even a distant one, who may possibly have been a…?"

"What?" Mel gasped. "A witch?"

Peter shrugged. "It's more common than most people think. You'd be surprised to know that most Anglo Saxons have a little of the witch in their genes."

"If I do have any of those genes, I'm afraid they must be dormant."

"They can always be reinvigorated with training and practice.".

"How would I know if I had any?"

"Well, being able to walk through the orchards and come out in one piece is a pretty good indication that there's some subconscious networking going on."

"That hardly sounds like definitive proof," Mel replied. "There must be some sort of test. Maybe if I could levitate some apples?"

"That would make you a magician, not a witch. Any talents that we have tend to be of a more cerebral nature rather than what's been depicted in movies."

"What about controlling the trees?" Mel insisted.

"Again, the trees were not being controlled. They were simply being asked to help," Peter answered.

Mel rolled her eyes.

"Why don't you try it?"

Mel gave him a confused look. "Try what?"

"See if you can communicate with the trees, or maybe with one tree as a start."

"What do I have to do?"

"The first thing is to completely empty your mind so that it's clear of clutter. Once that is done, you basically need to use that voice that all of us have in our head to start a dialogue."

"With a tree?"

"Initially, yes. Most find them the easiest life force to communicate with."

Mel waited until the pickers had completed the last minute clean-up of the area."

"Now?" she asked.

"Why not?"

Mel shook her head, knowing full well that what she was about to try was utterly absurd.

"Pick the closest tree and see what happens." He smiled encouragingly and stepped away from her.

Mel picked an exceptionally large and grand tree only a few metres from where she was standing. She spent a moment studying it, trying to imagine that it was far more sentient than a simple fruit-bearing tree. She stared at the trunk and the way it splayed at the bottom as its roots spread out beneath it.

For an instant, Mel was able to look at the parts of the tree, not as simple pieces of wood, but rather as a living entity and that the roots and branches were actually a complicated mass of intertwined muscles.

Mel took that last image as a sign that it was time for her to try and communicate. Peter stood silently behind her as she lowered her head and did her best to sweep away the mental detritus that was filling her consciousness.

She then waited until her ever-present inner voice revealed itself. It took a while before she sensed the voice ask her what she was trying to do.

Mel concentrated on trying to communicate with the tree, even though she felt ridiculous doing so.

Nothing happened.

After fifteen minutes of attempting to start a dialogue, Peter stepped up beside her. "Let me see if it's the tree or you."

Peter closed his eyes as Mel looked on with growing doubt.

After only a few seconds, Peter raised his head and shrugged. "I can communicate perfectly. Maybe you should get some sleep and give it another try tomorrow."

"Let me have a few more minutes, then I'll call it a night," Mel said.

"I'll wait with you."

"There's no need," she replied.

"I'll tell you what. I'll be in the shed checking on the packing from tonight's harvest. I'll swing by in about a half hour. If you haven't had any joy by that time, it's just possible that I was wrong about you."

Chapter 6

After thirty minutes, Mel hadn't seen nor heard any evidence that her communicating was working. She was about to give up when the nearest tree's upper branches began to rustle. She experienced a moment of pure euphoria until she saw that the same thing was happening to the other trees. A breeze had descended from the north of the orchard and animated the leaves and smaller branches of the trees. Faced with the reality that Peter's notion about her potential ancestry and latent powers was nothing more than either a wind-up or, more likely, a totally unfounded theory, she knew she had to give up.

Mel watched the apple trees for a few more minutes before deciding it was time that she headed back to the pub. She felt a strange excitement at having seen what the villagers were able to do, but at the same time, she was even more concerned about what exactly she could report back to the ministry.

Clearly, writing that the villagers have found a way to get the trees to assist in the harvesting was not an option. Mel decided that she would simply exaggerate the size of the cooperative workforce and focus on their long hours and obsessive obligation to get the fruit harvested, no matter what.

Mel was deep in thought when she heard it. She at first thought that the sound was something to do with the wind. She soon realised that the relatively gentle breeze could not be the cause of the din she was hearing.

It sounded like breaking branches and fast, thudding footfalls. What was even stranger was that the noise was either getting louder, or what was causing it was getting closer.

Before she could rationalise her growing fear, a figure emerged from the darkness. At first she couldn't recognise the man.

Then she did.

It was her supervisor, Brett Grant. His face was cut and his clothes were torn.

"Thank fuck!" he said as he stumbled towards her. "The bloke at the pub told me where you'd be, but trying to navigate through that bloody orchard at night was complete madness. Some of those trees are so close together I could hardly get past the lower branches. At one point, I could have sworn that they were actually reaching out for me."

"What are you doing here?" Mel said as she felt a lump of lead begin to form in her gut.

"I told you that I just might pop up for a little ... what should we call it? Extracurricular employee development?"

"You should go now," Mel stated flatly.

"I haven't come this far just to turn tail and head back to London. What say we head back to the pub? I've got a bottle of red in the car. We can have a nice drink in your room and see what happens."

"Brett, I've asked you nicely to please go. Nothing is ever

going to happen between you and me. Please don't make me bring HR into all this."

"Look, missy," Brett said as he stepped closer to her, "if you want to keep your job, your first priority is to keep me happy and stop making idle threats about HR. You know they will always side with management, so stop playing hard to get and let's you and me have a bit of a laugh."

Before Mel knew what was happening, Brett pulled her towards him and started kissing her. She was so shocked that at first she didn't even try to stop him. It wasn't until she felt his tongue trying to find its way between her teeth and his hand reaching between her legs that she reacted.

She raised her knee hard into his groin. Brett doubled over as he gasped for air.

"You had your chance you bitch," he seethed through gritted teeth. "Now I'm going to have to take what I want."

Mel watched in horror as Brett, in obvious pain, managed to straighten back up. Before she could even react, he pushed her to the ground and immediately straddled her waist.

"This would have been more fun if you'd played along, but trust me, I'll still enjoy it."

Mel tried to struggle, but between his weight on top of her and one hand around her throat, she could hardly move at all. Brett used his free hand to unzip her windbreaker, then rip open her t-shirt.

With her breasts exposed, Mel understood that Brett really did intend to rape her. Being unable to move, all she could do was to close her eyes and hide within her own mind, a trick she'd learned at school when students used to bully her about her weight or hair. If he planned to violate her, so be it, but she wasn't going to let herself be aware of what was going on.

Mel felt her mind clear as she sought out the sanctity of her inner self. Just as she was about to shut out the world entirely, Mel sensed a question float within her private space.

It asked simply, "Do you need help?"

For a microsecond, she opened the floodgates of her emotions and sensation, in effect, answering the question.

Before Mel could shut herself off again, she heard Brett scream as his weight was suddenly lifted from on top of her. She could hear the sound of leaves thrashing and wood rending all around her.

She opened her eyes and gasped as she saw Brett suspended a few metres away from her. He was entangled with branches from what looked to be dozens of different trees.

Mel got to her feet and rezipped her top. She stood watching her supervisor try to struggle his way out of their grasp, but it was clear that nothing could escape their tensile strength.

The most terrifying thing were his eyes. They were fixed on Mel, and even in his current predicament, she could see the hated burning within them. It was a rage bent on destruction.

Her destruction.

From somewhere deep within her subconscious mind another question surfaced.

"End problem?"

Mel stared into Brett's eyes and gave the question the only possible answer.

"Yes."

It was over in an instant. The moment she'd given her response, the branches tightened their grip then all pulled in a different direction.

Brett's body was ripped into countless pieces of torn flesh as his blood was strewn across a wide swatch of earth.

Mel felt she should look the other way but couldn't seem to do so. Instead, she watched intently as the ground soaked up the blood and the roots of the trees rose through the soil and dragged whatever parts were left of Brett down into the ground.

"I'd say you've proven me right," Peter said as he appeared beside Mel.

"What have I done?" she asked in a calm almost tranquil voice.

"Simply what had to be done. Besides, you didn't actually *do* anything, just a little coordinating."

"I didn't mean to," Mel replied.

"We could argue that detail for years. The important thing is that you protected yourself. The why and how, really isn't that important," Peter said.

"So, what happens now?"

"Life goes on."

"It's that simple?" Mel asked.

"It can be if you let it," Peter replied, smiling.

*

One year later, Mel was sitting in her office within the ministry, having just completed the employee evaluations for the staff members that reported directly to her. It was probably one of the most difficult tasks she had to do, ever since she'd been promoted to Brett's position when he'd … run off with no explanation.

There was a quiet knock on the door and one of the other new managers poked his head into her office.

"Come in."

"Someone left you a gift at security." Adam stepped into the room and held up a wicker basket covered with bright strips of multi-coloured cellophane.

"What is it?" Mel asked.

"I don't know, but it's bloody heavy."

"Sorry. Put it on the desk."

As Adam placed the basket next to her keyboard, their arms briefly touched, sending a ripple of pleasure through Mel. She'd only been out with him twice, but sparks were already flying between them.

"Well go on. See what's in there," Adam insisted.

Mel pulled the crinkly wrapping away and saw that she'd been sent apples. Glorious, red, plump apples. Tucked between the fruit and the wicker was a small white envelope.

"Looks like you have more than one admirer," Adam said with faux concern.

"Don't be silly. This is from the apple orchard I visited last year. They said they'd send me some of this year's harvest, but I didn't think they actually meant it."

"What does the note say?"

Mel opened it and removed a cream coloured piece of notepaper.

"It says that this year's crop is especially good. The apples from the east orchard are especially flavourful, and here's a sample."

Mel tried to keep a straight face as she recalled Peter's words on that night one year earlier when he promised to send some fruit from the trees in the area where Brett had met his end. Something about wanting her to understand the benefits of natural farming.

Mel reached for one of the apples and took a bite.

It was the sweetest piece of fruit she'd ever tasted.

LETHAL ASSIGNMENT

Chapter 1

Mike Gould couldn't remember how many people he'd killed.

There was a number on the screen, but that total only showed his stats for the past year. In reality, the figure was close to double what was on the leader board.

At sixteen years old, Mike was considered one of the best. His kills were clean, time specific and untraceable. His fee had increased over the past few years to the six figure bracket. He was worth it. He was that good.

Ever since his mom had died of the big C when he was ten, Mike had focused his anger and his grief on the online game *Lethal Assignment*. He'd given it a try at the urging of some of the kids at school and was immediately hooked.

The imagery and fluidity was completely life-like. All he had to do was wear one of the Intense Media headsets and he was fully equipped. There were no haptic gloves or virtual reality googles because everything was being generated by the users mind with a little electro-prompting from the software.

Even the headset was simple. It looked exactly like an off-the-shelf set of over-ear headphones, except attached to the headband was a third arm that angled forward, allowing a small, soft rubber nub to rest against the forehead.

All action was generated by the brain including all motion of the user's avatar. This allowed each player to become so immersed in the game environment that there was no conscious realisation that they were in fact creating the environment themselves.

Such was the realism that if, for example, you were supposed to be in Rome on assignment, then as far as your mind was concerned, you really were in Rome. Your perception, via your avatar, was as if you were walking around Italy's capital. Just as you could move your hand by subconsciously alerting the assigned motor neurons, your avatar's hand would move.

In addition, because the nuts and bolts of the game was memory-enhanced visualisation, the hand (or whatever other part you were looking at) was yours, right down to moles, scars or even missing digits. The only part of your body that was not perceivable were your sexual organs.

The game was, after all, aimed at teens and Intense Media did not want it to end up being used purely as a virtual sex reality, though rumours were rife that a sex version was in the works that would have age appropriate barriers to avoid misuse by anyone under eighteen.

Mike's friends had told him that there was no way that he could worry about anything else in life while playing the game. It transported the player into a completely believable alternate reality that was unimaginably fun and addictive.

The game itself was pretty simple; you put your name forward for specific assassination assignments, your avatar qualifies through a series of physical and mental tests, then, if you beat out everyone else, you get the contract.

Simple, right? The fun part was that it was up to the contract holder to plan every single stage of the killing. That included virtual visits to potential locations, weeks of watching the mark's movements and habits, and then (and only then) the assassin would decide on the method, the time and the location of the kill. On top of that, as a player rose in the ranking, he was trained, or rather his avatar was trained in every form of martial art, marksmanship, blade skill as well as endless classes on tracking, isolating and subduing the target. There was even one class called *Killing Like a Pro* where the top players were schooled on exactly what method of death to use in every conceivable situation.

Despite the game being only a virtual experience, the fact that everything was done though a cerebral interface meant that Mike experienced all the training and the classes as if he were right there in the thick of it.

There was a lot of shit in the media about the violence and the dark theme of the game, but compared to Grand Theft Auto or Call of Duty, Lethal Assignment was tame. Plus, having to plan each kill, sometimes from thousands of miles away, was enough of a challenge that players ended up learning a bunch of useful life skills.

Mike's biggest ambition was to usurp Nikita Blade from the number one spot. She (if her real-life controller really was a she) had been at number one for two years. She always got the primo assignments, some of which were rumoured to have hit the seven figure level.

Though Mike had spoken face to face (screen to screen) with other players, only avatars were used at all times. Player details were highly confidential, and though friends knew that other friends played the game, they kept their online personas completely secret. The only direct contact anyone had within the game was through Franco Gunn. He was the head of 'the agency' and basically ran the whole thing. He chose the finalists, picked the winners and gave out the red book.

The red book was the dossier containing everything about the target. There were lifelike photos of the mark, the family (if there was one), and where the person lived. There were also detailed data sheets which gave an astonishingly realistic background of the fictitious target.

Sometimes, if the hit was complex enough, the primary was permitted to enlist as many other hitters as he or she wanted, however, as each helper would share in the pay out, it was rare for anyone to use more than one other person, and even then, there had to be a damn good reason for not going it alone.

Mike, or Dallas Blofeld as he'd named his character, had only ever done solo kills. The rewards were greater, the planning was easier, plus there was the fact that if there was only one person running the hit, there was never a worry about what the other person was up to.

Dallas Blofeld's new kill assignment was relatively local. The mark, Tito Juarez, was a local enforcer for the Manolo crime family out of Colombia. The story was that he was thinking of changing his allegiance to a rival family. Dallas learned that the man was himself a stone cold killer and for most of the time kept a low profile with one exception.

Once a quarter, Tito would book a suite at Caesar's Palace in Las Vegas and spend three days playing hi-stakes poker and screwing hi-price escorts. It was the only time that he left Colombia and lowered his guard.

Tito believed that by flying in on a private jet and staying within the confines of the one hotel, he would remain safe. Caesar's Palace security was top notch and just getting a weapon inside the place was near impossible. When not gambling, Tito always used the same escort company that was renowned for their discretion and the vetting of their girls.

It took Mike (AKA Dallas) some serious due diligence before coming up with a workable plan. During one of his virtual site visits, he checked out the suite that Tito always booked. He had hoped to find somewhere to conceal himself within the room before the mark even checked in.

There was nowhere that Tito couldn't stumble upon by accident. Dallas sat down on the suite's king size bed and tried imagining the flow of the room once Tito arrived. He was getting frustrated by the lack of options when he let the heels of his shoes swing under the bed. They came in contact with solid wood.

Dallas checked all around it and found that the entire box spring was, in effect, a rectangular wood plinth. He tapped it and could hear the hollowness beyond. He lifted the mattress and saw that it lay upon a plywood base that had been covered in a dark green faux silk material so it fitted in with the room's decor.

Beneath the plywood was a void. The entire underside of the bed was an empty space enclosed by the wooden frame. It gave Dallas an idea.

Two days later, as Tito was being shown to his suite, Dallas

Blofeld lay within the under-mattress space, invisible to anyone else in the room. Usually, while lying in wait, he would be armed with the latest in assassination weaponry, all of which was available to buy with virtual money in the game's elaborate armoury, but because of the extreme hotel security, he'd chosen to go old-school. Pretending to be a member of the kitchen staff, he'd stolen a fourteen inch carving knife. He'd spent hours the previous day creating numerous slots through the silk wrapped plywood so that, when Tito was directly above one of them, he could slide the knife up and into his mark.

It was the first time that Mike's avatar was going to kill his designated target this up close and personal. Mike would have preferred to shoot the guy from a few hundred yards away, but recognised that his way was the only option under the circumstances. At the end of the day, so long as the virtual $750,000 ended up in his player gaming account, he didn't care.

Mike had hoped that Tito, once in the room, would decide to lay on the bed even if it was just for a few moments so that he could finish the job without having to spend any more time in the coffin-like box. Even though Dallas was under the bed, Mike's view of the site showed the utter blackness that surrounded his avatar and he started to feel a twinge of claustrophobia.

Suddenly, he could hear voices within the room. He found that if he pressed an ear to the wood frame, he could clearly hear what was being said. Mike had assumed that he would be shown the suite by the bellman but from what he was hearing, it was pretty obvious that Tito had brought one of his escorts up a little early.

"How come I haven't see you before?" Tito asked.

"I've been working out of Chicago for the past two years. I finally had enough of the shitty weather and thought I'd try some desert heat for a change."

"I can guarantee that I'll show you some heat," Tito replied, his voice coarse and aroused. "Come here."

"Don't you want to get to know each other a little?" the woman asked.

"Trust me, when I'm finished, you'll know me real good."

Mike could hear the distinct sound of noisy, wet kissing.

"Oh yeah," Tito's voice seemed to be an octave higher. "You make me so-"

The rest of his words were cut off by the sound of electrical sizzling.

Something heavy thudded to the floor.

Dallas shoved the mattress to the side and sprang to his feet. Standing in the middle of the room was a stunning blonde holding a hi-charge taser. In the other hand was a nasty looking curved blade that looked frighteningly like the velociraptor claw from the original *Jurassic Park* movie.

Tito was unconscious on the floor.

Dallas stared at the woman, who stared right back at him.

"Dallas Blofeld?" she asked.

"Nikita Blade?" Dallas asked right back.

Chapter 2

"What are you doing here? This is my assignment!" Nikita exclaimed.

"Bullshit. It's mine. I got the death warrant and the red book from Franco two weeks ago."

"Well, it looks like Franco is trying to double his chances, but you know the rules, the money goes to the one who completes the kill."

"Wait," Dallas said just as Nikita dropped to the floor and was about to jam her creepy weapon into Tito's throat. "We've both put a lot of time into planning this, why don't we mess with Franco and both take the guy out? Then we can split the fee and show the guy that he can't make the players turn on each other?"

"Why would I want to do that?" she asked. "I'm ten seconds away from keeping the whole one million."

"One million? He offered me seven hundred and fifty."

"That's kinda shitty," she said as she looked back down at Tito's neck.

"Don't you want to know what Franco's up to?" Dallas asked. "This is weird, secretly putting his two top contractors on the same hit."

"Yeah maybe, but … you know, I don't really care that much. I gotta start work on the next one. It's a major hit and

I could use the extra funds to set it up."

Dallas was about to say something when Nikita slid the sharp end under the man's chin and pulled the curved knife towards her.

Mike's view changed from the hotel room to the game's home screen just as Nikita Blade's score increased by a cool one million dollars.

"Fuck," he said as he took off the headset.

He couldn't believe that the game had actually fucked him over. What game does that. As much as he was pissed off at Franco, or whoever was really running the platform, he was also intrigued about the last thing that Nikita had said. She needed the money to fund a huge assignment.

What assignment?

Mike's avatar was in the same super-class as Nikita. If there was a big assassination in play, he would have been notified just like the other top earners. Mike put the headset back on and just by thinking of it, he activated a drop down menu. He selected *Open Assignments* then checked the box for the ones that were reserved for the top killers. There was no need for passwords or biometric verification as the software was already working in perfect sync with his brain.

There were only four A-list assignments waiting to go live. None of them was offering close to what Tito's assassination brought in. There was certainly nothing there that Nikita would have referred to as a major hit. That pissed him off even more. It meant that she had to have been offered the contract without having to go through the test phase with the other applicants.

Mike had never heard of that happening. Why would it?

It was the crux of the whole game. It was how a lesser killer could rise in the ranks. There were six categories of assassins. Newbies started at level six and worked their way up by completing assignments.

If they were going to start messing with the rules and giving certain players preferential treatment, the whole concept was going to go down the shitter. Mike decided that he wasn't going to take such an injustice and did what he always did when faced with a real life dilemma.

He sulked.

A few weeks later, Mike was stretched out on his bed looking to see if any new assignments had appeared on the site.

"Mike," his dad called from downstairs. "Dinner's ready."

When Mike's mom died and his dad became the chief chef, they found out, much to their disappointment, that he was so inept in the kitchen that he could, in fact, burn water. Mike fully expected to come down one day and find his father looking for the instructions on a box of cereal. With neither of them able to prepare anything that didn't involve a microwave and very explicit instructions, it was amazing that they didn't both starve.

Needless to say, mealtime was not something that either of them looked forward to. His dad did the best he could when he did their weekly shop, but even the most tempting frozen microwaveable dinner rarely lived up to the image on the pack or the description. Chicken Lo Mein with assorted Chinese vegetables took six minutes from frozen. At least that's what the packaging said, but even with the mid-bake stir and shake, the final product always ended up with parts that never seemed to receive the full blast of the electromagnetic radiation. If the noodles were fully cooked, the chicken bits would still have ice cold centres. Even if you threw it back in the microwave for a further few minutes, it only made things worse. Maybe the chicken was finally cooked through, but the noodles would be burned and hard enough to break teeth. No matter what they tried, nothing came out the way it should. Even a no-brainer like Lasagne ended up with an unpalatably cold and uncooked centre.

Mike walked down the stairs wondering what delectable offering was on that night's menu, and as he approached the kitchen, he sensed that something was wrong. There was no sound of the microwave buzzing along in the background, plus there was a weird smell in the hallway. It was a little like cooked food but had none of the plastic film odour that he had become used to.

The first thing he saw when he stepped into the kitchen was that the dining table was covered in food. Pork chops, mashed potatoes and green beans were all in separate foil containers. This was bizarre enough on its own but the thing that really messed with his head was that the table was set for three.

"Sit down, Mike. We're having real food for a change."

Before Mike could enquire how such a thing was even possible, he heard the powder room door open in the hallway. A few moments later Becky White stepped into the room. She was taller than Mike, wore her hair in a bob, and even at thirty-eight, still had no wrinkles. Instead, a cluster of freckles covered the bridge of her nose and upper cheek bones.

Mike knew every single one of those wrinkles. Every able bodied guy at school knew them, knew her green eyes, her tom-boy figure and her shapely legs. Miss White probably starred in more pubescent fantasies than anyone cared to imagine.

"Isn't this nice," his dad said. "Miss White's brought us dinner."

"Why?" The question came out of Mike's mouth before his brain even kicked in.

"I thought you'd like a home cooked dinner for a change," Becky answered.

"Wasn't that nice of her?" Mike could hear the urgency in his dad's voice.

"Unless you are dropping off dinner at ever other student's house, I can't help thinking that there's a scary back-story to you being here, Miss White."

"Call me Becky, please."

"Okay... so did you drop off food at every other student's home ... Becky?"

"No, Mike. I did not," she replied calmly. "Yours is the only one."

"May I ask why we are so blessed?"

"Michael. Don't be rude," his father said, trying to take control of the situation.

"Don't worry, Ron. Mike and I have a good long standing working relationship."

Mike assumed that by good relationship, she meant that whenever he disagreed with her in class, he somehow ended up in detention.

"Mike, I think you're old enough to understand what I'm

going to tell you," Becky continued, smiling.

"Becky, are you sure this is the best time?" Ron said, still believing that he had any skin in the game.

"Mike, your father and I have been seeing each other for a few months now. We've kept it very low key, but recently, it's become serious."

Mike thought he was going to puke. His teacher had, on many occasions, been front and centre in his own erotic fantasies. Though there were a few girls in his show reel, Miss White was always on top ... so to speak. Now, she was sleeping with his dad. Mike didn't even know what psychological philosophy that would fit into, but it was bound to be one where the poor deluded son ends up in therapy for the rest of his life.

"I gotta go," Mike said before grabbing his jacket and running out into the twilight, making sure to slam the door as hard as he could.

Chapter 3

The big problem with living in a small town like Mesquite was that, when faced with a dramatic exit from one's home, there was nowhere to storm off to. There were no malls, amusement parks or anywhere else where self-respecting teens would hang out. The town did, however, have a mega marijuana dispensary which resulted in Mesquite having an above average number of Ice cream parlours.

Mike decided on Cones on Sandhill Blvd.

The only thing to be said for the place was that it was usually empty. That night was no exception. Mike sat at one of the counter stools and ordered a chocolate malt with an extra shot of chocolate syrup.

No matter how much he wanted to appear to be the strung out, misunderstood bad boy of the small town, he didn't drink, do drugs or smoke and by ordering an extra shot for his malted shake, he was pretty much cementing his reputation for being a good student and all around lame ass.

About the time that his shake was placed in front of him, the staff had stopped what they'd been doing and were gawking at the flat screen TV that usually only showed the Weather Channel. A program about how tornados were formed was interrupted by a news alert.

The President of the World Bank had been assassinated

while on a visit to Spain. He'd been getting out of his car in front of the Hotel Fenix Gran Meliá in Madrid, when what appeared to be a passer-by, pointed a silenced handgun only inches from his head and had fired twice. The assailant, who appeared to be wearing a full Hijab and veil, bowed once, then had almost magically vanished into the gathering crowd. Grainy footage showed the moment the assassination took place.

Mike was able to determine two things almost immediately. The shooter used a Heckler and Koch, VP9 Tactical OR. It was a pro's gun and very few people used it. It was impossible to see who the shooter was, but there was something about the stance, the fluidity of motion and especially the bowing that looked awfully familiar.

Mike was about to turn back to his shake when a new banner glided by in the lower third.

GUNMAN APPREHENDED was the headline. As he read the moving text, he saw that it had been a young local man. Beyond that, there was no more information.

When Mike got home, his father was waiting for him in the living room. Alone.

At first he expected to take a lot of shrapnel over his uncool departure, but instead, his dad just wanted to make sure that Mike was alright. They ended up talking for over an hour (a new home record). It seems that his dad had been deeply worried that Mike wouldn't understand his getting serious over a woman other than his mother. Mike convinced him that five years was enough time to mourn her and that he was happy that he'd found someone. The fact that Miss White was his teacher was definitely a bit weird, but if someone was going to be spending serious time within the Gould household, it might as well be Becky.

Mike flopped down on his bed and checked for upcoming assignments. Strangely there were none. He was about to log off when something made him check the kill leader board. Nikita Blade's earnings had gone up by two million dollars.

Mike was furious; he was one of the top players in the world and hadn't even been notified of the highest paying contract, ever. What was really frustrating was that there were no details on the hit that had earned her all that virtual cheddar.

After spending a while stewing in the safety of his own mind, Mike decided that he had every right to question the new procedural quirk. He started to compose a message on the game's 'contact us' screen when Nikita's position on the leader board changed. Actually, change wasn't the right word. Her name and earnings simply vanished.

As number two on the board, Mike's avatar was automatically moved up to the top of the ranking. Dallas Blofeld was now the best online assassin in the *Lethal Assignment* universe.

While that was a major achievement, Mike couldn't help wondering what had happened to Nikita's stats. He'd never seen someone erased from the board. Uncomfortable with his unexpected position, Mike checked Nikita's profile to see if there were any changes that could explain her fall from the top slot.

She was gone. There was no one on the assassin list called Nikita Blade. Mike checked a number of chat rooms on the site where he knew she'd been involved in some dialogues, but there was no record of her ever having existed on the platform. Even her avatar's paid sponsorship ads for various weapons or accessories had all gone.

A drop down appeared on his iPad showing that there were additional news feeds on the Madrid assassination. Mike opened the string and saw that the main trending report was that the killer was claiming that he had been completely unaware that he was shooting anyone. He knew that he'd been seen by dozens of people and that the gun he'd been holding was the murder weapon, but he was adamant that he had nothing to do with it.

Alvar Soheit ran a small kabab restaurant next to the train station. The last thing he remembered was sitting in his studio apartment playing video games.

Mike clicked on one of the news sites that had an interactive component and asked one simple question: What games had he been playing?

It took over half an hour for the service to wade through thousands of newsfeeds to find that snippet that only a few agencies had bothered to mention.

The reply said: *Mortal Kombat* and *Zombie Apocalypse*.

"Crap," Mike thought to himself.

Then another game was added.

Lethal Assignment.

Mike felt a chill run the entire length of his body, though he wasn't sure why. Sure, the killer had been playing L.A. but so were millions of others around the world. He was more concerned with what had happened to Nikita than worrying about some guy who was obviously trying to play the crazy card to avoid a firing squad or whatever the hell they do in Spain.

Mike continued with his message. He addressed it to Franco Gunn hoping that there actually was such a person, and that, if he did exist, he'd bother to read one of what had to be thousands of messages a day.

Mike basically asked what happened to Nikita, and why other assassins were not offered the chance to compete for the last big pay-out contract. Mike then logged out of his tablet and was even considering doing some homework when a loud barking sound filled his room. That was his chosen sound for all incoming texts or emails.

He powered up the iPad screen and saw that he had a message response from Franco Gunn.

The reply was a link to a URL that Mike didn't recognise.

Mike might not have known the address but he certainly knew where it was located.

It was a URL for the dark web.

Below the address were the words: connect at 17:55 MST.

Mike looked at the time at the top of the iPad screen.

It was 17:54.

Mike clicked the link at the exact second that the iPad clock showed 17:55. His screen went black, then went all analogue, with wavy lines, random static and snow. He was about to disconnect and try again when the noise and grain on the screen formed into a face.

At first it looked like one of the stone heads on Easter Island but after a few seconds it settled on what appeared to be a distorted image of Abraham Lincoln. As if that wasn't strange enough, the face had a weird Max Headroom stutter effect going on.

"You contacted me about Nikita Blade," the twitching head spoke in a voice that was as distorted as the image.

"Franco Gunn?" Mike asked.

"Tha...tha...that's me," Franco's image replied sounding just a little too much like Elmer Fudd.

"You read my message?"

"Yes."

Mike waited, expecting more of an answer.

"So, why weren't the other Level 1 assassins offered the chance to bid of the last contract? Why did Nikita get it without having to complete the challenge?"

"She got a special deal," Franco replied.

"Was being removed from the game part of the special deal?" Mike asked.

Franco's head just sat there shuddering.

"Where is Nikita?"

"Gone."

"That's not good enough," Mike snapped back. "I want to know..."

The head seemed to turn a dark crimson as the twitching increased.

"Nikita is gone," it stated coldly. "That's all you need to know. There is no more Nikita. You are the new leader and you will be receiving the next select assignment."

"What does select assignment mean?" Mike asked. "I've never heard of that?"

"That's because you have only now become number one. You will receive your offer within twenty-four hours."

Mike wanted to ask a gillion more questions but the screen zeroed out to a bright dot like on old analogue televisions, then went black.

The next day was Saturday. Usually a day without school was the best thing ever, but that was before Mike's dad began bringing school into the house. As a 'wonderful' surprise for Mike, Becky showed up at seven in the morning, or at least that was what they both said. If they wanted to pretend that Miss White hadn't spent the night, they should have kept the grunting down to a much lower level.

The plus side was that Miss White was an excellent cook, and this particular Saturday morning was the first in a long, long time that he was served a real breakfast.

"Look Mike, Becky came by early to fix us some breakfast," his dad said, beaming.

Mike desperately wanted to reply with something snarky but decided not to screw up blueberry pancakes and extra crispy bacon.

He was on his second stack of pancakes when he heard the dogs barking up in his room.

He had a message.

With looks of concern from the love birds, Mike scarfed down the freshly buttered and syruped starchy discs like a starving wolverine, then charged upstairs.

There was a drop down message that simply said: check site.

Mike considered himself to be pretty technically minded, but for the life of him, he couldn't work out how the drop down had originated. They were almost always iOS system reminders for version updates and stuff. They were never used for messaging, yet not only was there a drop down message, it had triggered the barking text alert.

Mike logged into Lethal Assignment and was stunned to see an entirely new home screen. It was as if he was logging in to a completely different game. Gone were the cool graphics and links to the various sub-platforms. It was basically just a black screen with gold lettering that invited the user to log in. Mike put on the headset and was automatically logged on. Another screen opened. This one was entirely customised to him. It even had a welcome message:

DALLAS, WELCOME TO LEVEL X.

The page had none of the glitz of the original game pages. Instead it looked like a temporary web design. Out of curiosity, mike checked the URL and saw that it was a dark web address that bore no relation to the old one he'd been using for years.

There were a lot of links to the same accessories and support but everything had a cheap HTML feel to it. As he studied the page, a gold coloured envelope appeared mid-screen. On it was a big X and nothing else. Mike clicked on it and the envelope unfolded revealing a contract similar to the fake looking ones used in the regular part of the game. The difference with this one was the number on the bottom. Mike had never seen a number like it on the game. It was twice the amount that Nikita had earned for her last kill.

The weird thing was that there was no mention of the target. The end of the page simply had two boxes. One said: PROCEED. The other said: RETURN TO BASIC GAME. Mike stared at the two buttons, then pressed the first one.

Chapter 4

A dossier appeared.

On the front cover was the picture of an Arab man wearing a white, ankle-length thobe and a red and white checked keffiyeh on his head. He was standing on the stern of a mega yacht talking to two westerners, both wearing expensive looking suits. The photo looked to have been taken from a long distance.

The name underneath was Sheik Osama Shams al-Din. Mike had never heard of him. Then again, he rarely knew who the targets were. Presumably because their identities were entirely fictitious and had been created by the game's algorithm. Even the photos were fake. Mike knew there was no Sheik Osama Shams al-Din and that the likeness was nothing more than a generic CGI mash-up from the game's massive data library.

Mike accepted the assignment and immediately began researching the mark on L.A.'s website. As always, the data trail was extensive, making his planning far easier than would be the case in the real world. Mike could see where the Sheik lived, where he ate, who he fucked and who he was fucking over. On a side screen, Mike started making notes while he searched for patterns in the guy's habits and actions. That was key to finding the weak spots. It didn't matter how much security they surrounded themselves with if once a week they ditched the protection team so they could satisfy some private urge.

After two weeks of searching Mike finally found the anomaly. Every two weeks, on Saturday afternoon at five o'clock, the Sheik drove himself in a generically invisible car from his compound near the Champs Elysée in Paris to a small apartment block in the 11th arrondissement.

Mike had no idea what he did there, but at least he knew where he'd be at a specific time on a specific date. He booked his virtual travel on the site and after flying first class on Air France, Dallas Blofeld landed at Charles de Gaulle international airport. He used one of his many passports to clear immigration then took the airport bus to the centre of Paris.

As travelling with a firearm was near impossible even in the virtual world, Mike had decided to use a much more covert method to terminate the mark. In his carry-on bag, he carried two vials of insulin and a five-day supply of single use syringes.

If asked about the contents of the glass vials, he would produce his medical ID card showing that he was a diabetic. Nobody ever seemed to dig any deeper which was a good thing. Dallas had no trouble with his blood sugar levels. In the vials was a highly concentrated batrachotoxin that was strong enough to wipe out a small town.

Dallas booked into the George V Hotel and treated himself to the most expensive room service meal he could find, deciding to let his avatar splurge considering the massive amount of virtual coin the guy was about to earn.

Dallas spent his time wandering around Paris like any other tourist, waiting for his moment. As it approached three o'clock, he focused his attention on finding his mark.

To avoid any possibility of leaving a trail by using public transport, Dallas walked the nine kilometres to the 11th arrondissement. He arrived with forty minutes to spare and spent that time familiarising himself with the narrow street and the entrance to the apartment building where the Sheik visited on a bi-weekly basis.

Most killers would hit the target on his way into the building but Mike (and therefore Dallas) knew that people were always more apprehensive upon arrival at a destination and were usually far more at ease and thus less aware of their surroundings upon leaving the same premises.

The data showed that the mark always stayed less than an hour. Whatever he did in the building seemed to require a very specific amount of time.

The other advantage of waiting to hit the guy on the way out was that Dallas would know where the sheik had parked and could position himself accordingly.

The Rue Basine was narrow and only had parking on one side. There was one available space and it was a good hundred or so metres from the apartment entrance.

Across the street from the parking space was a small neighbourhood park. At that time of day, there was hardly anyone within it. Dallas found a bench that gave him a clear view of the street, the parking place and the building. All he had to do was watch and wait.

At three minutes before five, a nondescript grey Renault

184

turned into the Rue Basine and pulled into the empty parking place. Dallas pretended to be looking at his phone screen but behind his mirrored glasses, he had his eyes glued to the car.

The Sheik wasn't wearing any of his usual tradition Arab garb. Instead, he had gone for jeans and a T-shirt. If Dallas hadn't known who he was, the man would have blended easily into the diaspora of the giant city.

With a baseball cap pulled down covering his eyes, Sheik Osama was all but invisible as he walked with casual ease towards the apartment.

Dallas, not wanting to be seen in exactly the same position when the man emerged from the building, walked to the end of the street and waited patiently.

Fifty-eight minutes later, Sheik Osama headed back to his car. He felt relaxed, yet invigorated. Ever since his relationship with Tommy, a young German teen, had turned to a regular physical encounter, he had found himself counting the days and minutes till the next meeting.

A pedestrian bumped into him, apologised profusely, then walked off. He shrugged it off and continued walking, but when he reached his car he realised he couldn't seem to catch his breath. He began clawing at his throat as his face turned an ever darkening shade of greyish blue.

He fell to his knees and tipped forward with his head coming to rest against the four year old Renault.

The avatar's image of Paris went black for a millisecond after which the word CONGRATULATIONS appeared in gold lettering accompanied by cheesy fanfare music and an animated explosion of party balloons and confetti.

Mike could never understand why the designers had thought to have such a dumb-ass graphic at the end of a successful hit. It was more like what you'd expect if you reached the top level of Candy Crush, not as a result of successfully killing someone.

Mike didn't care.

He was four million virtual dollars richer. As far as he was concerned, they could show dancing bears on pogo sticks.

The next day, his dad and Becky were mid-conversation when Mike walked into the living room. The TV was on Fox news which drove him insane, but no matter how many times he'd tried to get his dad to understand that half of what they were peddling was pure, grade A bullshit, his dad just wouldn't believe him. Mike thought of the old, tweaked adage: 'You can lead a guy to slaughter but you can't make him think'.

Both adults stopped talking.

"What's going on?" Mike asked.

"Nothing. Just some unpleasant news from Europe," Becky said.

"Anything that's going to affect my life?" Mike queried.

"Not unless you suddenly give a damn about the Saudi economy," his dad replied. "Their minister of finance dropped dead earlier today."

Mike shrugged as he started towards the kitchen.

"They found the poor man crumpled on the ground in a lovely looking street in the middle of Paris," Becky added.

Mike felt a chill spread throughout his body. Sure, it could be unrelated, but what were odds of an important Arab dying in Paris only hours after he'd virtually killed a similar mark online?

It had to be some weird coincidence.

"They've arrested some woman who was found across the street from where it happened."

"Why?" Mike asked.

"She was just sitting there with a syringe in her hand mumbling about not understanding what she'd done. The police think she may have injected the minister with poison or something."

Mike continued into the kitchen just so the others couldn't see the look on his face. Some of the blocks were starting to fit into place. Nikita had scored the biggest contract he ever heard of then the Head of the World Bank gets assassinated in Madrid by some guy who doesn't even know what fucking day it is.

Next, Mike gets an even bigger contract, completes the kill, then another VIP turns up dead in the same city where his virtual assignment took place. And again, some poor nobody is arrested even though they haven't got a clue what the hell's going on.

Mike suddenly had a very strange thought. He ran upstairs, accessed his online newsfeed and checked for more details on the woman who'd been arrested. He found footage that someone had filmed on their phone of her actually being arrested. As she was bundled into a French Police van, she was screaming something in French. Mike did an audio grab of her voice then put it through Google translate. As he read the interpreted words, his blood ran cold. She was screaming that she was innocent and had been at home playing a video game and had no idea how she ended up in the park. When asked what game had she been playing by a paparazzo, she answered, "Lethal Assignment".

Mike felt a wave of nausea as it dawned on him that somehow, though inadvertently, he was involved with the latest real world killing.

Two low level players were being accused of assassinating some seriously important real-world people, one in Madrid, the other in Paris. That was bad enough, but Mike knew that he had been controlling his hit via Dallas: an avatar. There was no way he could have been controlling... Mike looked at the woman's name again. Estelle LaFleur. Besides, the whole thing was virtual. None of the marks were real. The whole thing was just elaborate make-believe, right?

Mike was about to turn off his iPad when he noticed that his home screen had changed. He was now looking at the login screen for first time users. WTF. He was hardly a first time user. He was numero uno. Frustrated, but curious, he entered his username and password.

A message appeared that said simply: Location confirmed.

Mike wondered what that could possibly mean considering the game was completely secure and confidential. The monthly membership fee was paid with bitcoin and nowhere was there any contact information like an address or phone number.

He was about to reboot the pad when he smelled something unusual.

Gas. He smelled gas.

He ran out of his room and sensed that it was stronger on the landing. As he started downstairs, it got full-on pungent. Mike covered his mouth with his T-shirt to try and keep some of the fume's potency at bay. Becky and his dad were still in the living room but looked as if they'd gone to sleep on the sofa. It took some serious shaking and screaming to get them to open their eyes and look up at him with confused expressions.

With him in the middle, he managed to get both of them to the front door, then out onto the tiny square of green that was all the front lawn they could manage in the desert town.

Mike took a couple of deep breaths of clean air as the other two coughed their guts up a few feet away.

Then the house exploded.

Chapter 5

The blast knocked Mike off his feet. He felt as if he'd been hit by a charging elephant. It was a good job that his dad and Becky were already on the ground. All the blast did to them was roll them over a few times.

When the smoke cleared, he saw that the only home he'd ever known was gone. All that was left was some smouldering debris and part of the brick chimney that had somehow remained upright. What was left of the house and their belongings was scattered across a twenty yard radius.

Mike felt as if his head was filled with cotton balls and the ringing in his ears was deafening. He gave himself a quick check-over and found that he didn't seem to have any serious injuries, though his favourite vintage Led Zeppelin T-shirt was torn and looked to be singed in places.

Mike crawled over to the others and was relieved to see that they were no worse for wear. Having been lying down flat at the time of the explosion was a stroke of luck. Wedged into the grass only five feet behind them was their washing machine, one corner of which was buried a good few inches into the lawn. Mike figured that if either of them had been standing up, the appliance would have done some serious harm.

Mike, Becky and Ron just sat there, not knowing what

else to do. Neighbours had emerged from their houses and were making their way over. A couple of sirens could be heard in the distance. Mesquite might have been a small town, but thankfully it had a decent hospital, ambulance service and fire department. They would all be needed that night.

The three were admitted to Mesquite General for 'observation' which was doctor speak for: 'we don't have a clue what's wrong with you, so let's just watch and see if something starts to bleed or fall off.'

An overnight stay in a hospital is not a relaxing affair. It seemed to Mike that every frigging time he started to doze off, someone would wake him up so they could take his temperature and poke him in a whole lot of places.

The next morning, Mike was cleared to leave but his dad and Becky were told that they had to stay a little longer. Becky was having trouble breathing which could have been the smoke, the gas fumes or both. His dad couldn't keep any food or water down which apparently happens when you get a decent dose of gas poisoning.

Mike wandered out into a glaringly bright day and saw the town Sheriff, Jeff Hurst, leaning against his police SUV. Jeff was a long-time family friend of the Goulds.

"Feel like talking?" Jeff asked.

"Sure. I can honestly say that I have nowhere else to go." Mike replied.

"Ben over at the ERA office has loaned your family one of his personal rental properties. It's usually on the BnB sites, but he's just had it recarpeted and painted. It's only a townhouse but it's fully furnished and it'll suit until you guys

191

get yourselves sorted out."

Mike thanked him as he got into the passenger seat. He was happy it was Jeff that had chosen to come by.

Mike had assumed that they would make for the Sheriff's office on the other side of town, but instead, Jeff drove straight to the town's only Denny's.

"I thought you'd be hungry, plus I didn't see the need to get all sheriffy with you and have our talk in our interview room."

"Thanks," Mike said, smiling.

Once they were seated in the back booth and had placed their orders, Jeff asked the expected first question.

"So what the fuck happened?"

Mike told him everything he knew except for the part about his possibly being responsible for somehow killing a man in Paris.

"They're sending someone from the Vegas Fire Department to survey the site, but Tim over at the local station is pretty sure why the house blew up. The gas line to the stove wasn't even attached to the wall valve. The house must have been full of fumes. The question is why wasn't the stove attached?"

Mike just shrugged. "Could it have fallen off?"

Jeff shook his head. "For obvious reasons, it's designed not to do that. It even had one of those new fool proof IP security collars on it so that it could be monitored from the gas company. We have to wait to hear what the inspector says, but right now it looks as though the collar somehow failed."

Mike had already come to the realisation that the

explosion had been an attempted hit, but he sure as shit wasn't going to tell that to the sheriff. The questions stopped as the food was spread out before them. Jeff waited until they were alone before continuing.

"Can you think of anyone who might have wanted to harm any of you?"

"Of course not. As far as I know, none of us has ever had that sort of enemy." Mike decided to throw a red herring into the mix. "What about Becky … Miss White? There could easily be some student from her past that's been holding a grudge or whatever."

"Then why not attack her when she's alone?" Jeff asked.

"Dude, I'm just spit balling here. How the hell would I know who the fuck blew up our house? The worst we've ever experienced was a toilet paper attack last summer."

Jeff seemed to divert his interest in Mike to the plate of food in front of him.

"I hope you know that I had to ask those questions," he said as he forked half a sausage into his mouth.

"I know you did," Mike replied.

"I'm just trying to put some pieces together here."

"I know you are."

Neither spoke as they ate.

After what seemed like an eternity, Jeff said, "Do you want me to drop you off at Ben's townhouse after this?"

"Is Kenny at home today?" Mike asked.

"Well, you know my son. Always locked in that basement cave of his."

Mike was already starting to put the puzzle pieces together. His situation might have been pretty unique in the real world, but on the gaming platform, eliminating virtual witnesses or co-conspirators was relatively standard.

The game had taught him everything he needed to know about assassination. For them to try and wipe him off the face of the platform and planet was a stupid play. Mike now had no choice but to turn all his lethal abilities against whoever had made the move against him and his family. Though he had no idea who could be behind it, Mike knew where to start.

Once he and Kenny got past the obligatory small talk, Mike asked casually, "You still playing Lethal Assignment?"

"If you call being a sixer an assassin, then yes, but all I get to do is fight for some shitty scraps that might roll downhill from the higher groups."

"You just have to persevere. Do you mind logging in and going to the earnings page? I want to check something out."

Kenny, a semi-friend who seemed to be permanently trying to emulate an early Keanu Reeves look, opened a new browser tab, logged in then clicked the menu option. As Mike feared, Dallas Blofeld was no longer on top, in fact he wasn't on the leader board at all. Just like Nikita, the moment the 'select' hit was completed, all traces of his avatar had vanished.

"That's weird," Kenny mumbled. "Where are Nikita and Dallas? I don't think I've ever looked at this screen without one of those two being at the top."

"Yeah," Mike agreed. "That's pretty weird."

Mike let a moment of time elapse.

"Do you still have that old, peddle-powered IBM?"

"It's not that old, and yes, I keep it in case I need to do a Beowulf Cluster."

"Do you still have that first gen L.A. headset?"

"I have it, but I don't know if it still works."

"Can I borrow them?"

Alone in the townhouse, Mike cooked himself a frozen pizza that Jeff had included in a bag of essentials he'd put together from his own home. Thankfully, as the townhouse was usually a VRBO property, it had great Wi-Fi.

He felt a little guilty about what he was planning to do, but he needed some of the Lethal Assassin tools which were no longer available to him as his account had been deleted. He needed to use Kenny's avatar to research one particular location. His plan was that if he followed the Avatar's exact movements, he could replicate everything he learned in real life.

He opened the L.A. login screen and was embarrassed for his friend. Not only did Kenny have his username and password on autoload, which was so uncool for such a site, but Mike learned that he'd named his avatar Keanu. It wasn't exactly a shock, but come on.

Keanu had just enough virtual coin in his account to fly from Vegas to Portland Oregon then drive a non-descript rental car to the town of Newport. Mike had found the house he was looking for on Google maps so, though he didn't have an exact address, he knew how to get there.

Two miles north of the town, a private road led towards the coast. Keanu left the car at a scenic pullover a little way beyond the turn off then doubled back. The road was less than a quarter mile long and dead-ended at the forecourt of the famed home of Christopher Gables: founder of Intense Media and creator of the Lethal Assignment game.

The house looked like a pair of giant silver wings that were spread perching over the side of a sheer cliff. Mike had seen a million pictures of the place but viewing it with his own eyes … or at least virtually through Keanu's own eyes, was a whole different experience. The photos never gave the structure the scale it deserved. The place was huge. With the sun glinting off the etched chrome roofing, it almost looked like a giant prehistoric avian about to soar off the cliff top.

Keanu suddenly stopped dead and the image began to blur. The avatar couldn't get any closer. The house was only virtually visible because Gables allowed the players that limited access. He probably coded it in so that the lowly plebs could get a glimpse of his wealth without running the risk of them being able to actually snoop around.

Mike logged out of the game and went to YouTube and searched *Volo D'Argento*, the name of the estate. He found dozens of videos shot from the beach, looking directly up at the dramatic house. Mike wasn't looking to admire the structure; he was looking for a way in.

Chapter 6

Mike stood on the coast road and bundled his windbreaker around him. It must have been blowing over twenty knots, and unlike Arizona at that time of year, it was actually cold. He should have brought more clothes, but Becky and his dad thought he was just going to St George to stay with a friend for a couple of days. Mike hoped that his dad wouldn't check his Amex bill for a while because the flight to Oregon plus the rental car wasn't exactly cheap. Mike had only ever booked travel on the game site and wasn't aware of all the penalties involved with last minute travel.

He made his way down a public path to the beach, then headed south. It was a fifteen minute walk along the shoreline until he was standing directly under *Volo D'Argento*. From his angle, tucked close into the cliff-side, it wasn't that beautiful. The tons of steel and concrete that were needed to support the monolith appeared functional without any attempt at beautifying its structural integrity.

Mike found what he was looking for. In the YouTube videos there'd been a visible gantry suspended under an oversized, central steel girder. He assumed that it was there for inspection and repair purposes. Because of its location, Mike could see that there was no way to get to it from either side of the building. The only possibility was that there had to be an access hatch or doorway that led from inside the house itself.

Though rock climbing hadn't been part of his curriculum, Mike spent the previous night watching a gazillion YouTube videos showing the basics of what to do. The day was getting colder and the beach was deserted which was a good thing. Having someone alert the police that a strange kid was trying to climb up towards Christopher Gables' house would have been extremely problematic.

The cliff wasn't completely vertical which helped. It was however soft in areas where layers of sand had been deposited over the millennia. After a few embarrassingly flawed starts, Mike got the hang of it. The hardest part was finding the right toe holds. Though the video made it look downright easy, that was not the case in the real world.

Despite the cold and the strengthening wind that was coming in off the slate-grey Pacific, Mike was sweating up a storm. His T-shirt was drenched and it was starting to seep into his fleece.

By the time he reached the halfway point, his legs and arms were trembling from exertion. He stopped and after managing to find some close approximation of a ledge, he just leaned into the cliff as he gathered enough strength to finish the climb.

Mike was about to continue his ascent when, out of the corner of his eyes, he saw a dark shadow dropping towards him. Before he could even react, it stopped right next to him. Mike's first thought was that it was a boulder or maybe even some sort of home defence system that automatically dropped explosive charges on approaching enemies. The object turned out to be a human wearing a repelling harness. Mike tensed himself for what he assumed was going to be a cliff-face confrontation when the person removed their thermal, silk balaclava from their head.

It was a girl. She was maybe in her mid to late teens and was obviously of east Asian descent though she looked as if she may have had western genes somewhere in the mix. One thing that was very clear was that she looked both furious and anxious at finding Mike halfway up the cliff.

"You have to jump now," she stated.

"Are you out of your mind?" Mike replied. "Who the hell are you anyway?"

"The person who's going to save your dumb ass," she said as she reached across and with frightening ease, plucked Mike from his perch, sending him screaming towards the beach, forty feet below.

Because of the sand accumulation at the bottom, the landing was sloped and lessened the force of the impact. All the same, Mike's breath was knocked out of him and his ankle felt torqued. A coil of climbing rope landed next to him, followed only moments later by the young woman. She grabbed him by the collar of his windbreaker and practically dragged him down the beach. Finally, Mike was able to get his legs out from under him and ran alongside her, despite the growing pain in his ankle.

Once they'd covered about a hundred yards, she stopped and looked back towards the house. From the new angle, it looked even more like a giant bird about to push off into the sky.

Standing on the structure's cantilevered terrace were

two men, staring down at them.

"Fuck," Mike said. "That's him. That's Gables. I was so close. Why the fuck did you have to stop me?"

The girl looked up at the men then checked her steel diver's watch. She smiled as she looked back at them again. Mike was about to ask her what the hell was going on, when she dropped to one knee and bowed towards the two men.

A shiver ran through every fibre of Mike's body. He'd seen that gesture many times in the kill replays used to train other online assassins.

"Nikita?" Mike stammered.

She looked over at Mike and winked. Then the clifftop exploded in flame. For a brief moment, the giant bird looked as if it really was going to be able to fly up and away from the conflagration. Instead, it began to crumble into a falling heap of concrete, wood, glass and steel.

"We should go," Nikita stated.

"You are her aren't you?" Mike asked.

"My avatar is Nikita. I am Lila Chang," she said with a slight bow. "And you are Mike Gould, creator of the avatar Dallas Blofeld."

"How did you … I don't understand."

"I am a few days ahead of you in tracking down and killing those that came after me … us. My mother was killed when they attacked my home."

"But how do you know about me?"

"Christopher Gables was my second target since they came for me. My first was the man behind the Franco Gunn avatar. Before he died, I was able to learn a great deal. When I found out that you too had been targeted, I planned to look for you after this mission."

"Why?"

"Because with two of us, we stand a better chance of destroying their entire operation before they have control of the world's financial centres," Lila replied.

"But you just ended it. Christopher Gables is dead. What more is there to do?" Mike asked.

"Gables and Lethal Assignment were just the tools. Others were ordering the hits. You and I have a lot of work ahead of us before we and the rest of the world can be safe. So, to answer your question, no, this isn't the end. This..." Lila gestured to the flaming wreckage that was draped down the side of the cliff, "...is just the beginning."

They drew closer together as they watched the carnage she had caused. Mike felt a moment of pride mixed with excitement at having teamed up with Lila, then things began to change.

The cliffside began to look like a bad video signal on his TV at home. Data blocks began to appear, then separate, lifting the entire image up, and out of sight.

He turned to Lila and could tell from her expression that she'd seen the same thing. As he looked into her eyes they too began to fill with digital artifacts.

"What happening t-" Mike started to ask, but his voice sounded like it was going through auto-tune as the different layers of his voice's harmonics began to shift frequency.

The beach and even the ocean turned to sparkling digitized specs which rose in the air then vanished completely, leaving behind a flat blue background.

Mike and Lila reached for each other but their arms

began to disintegrate.

Within a basement many thousands of miles from where Mike and Lila thought they had existed, a man sat in front of an array of flat screens.

He watched as his two lead characters pixelated into digital oblivion and red text filled the screen.

GAME OVER.

LIGHT DUSTING

Chapter 1
(2007)

Peter Wellings sat silently with the other witnesses within the State Prison in Northern Florida. He was the only member of his family that chose to be there that day. The others had broken off all connection with his brother, Bill, from the moment he'd been found guilty of murdering Diana Everett almost three years earlier.

Diana's body had been found by an Everglades tour guide. She had washed up against a mangrove thicket and her arms had become ensnared within the exposed roots. The man had at first thought she was a mannequin until he realised that they don't make those with a grey-green skin colour.

After examining hours of traffic camera footage, the police found a video of Diana getting into a dark green Chevy Malibu only a few a hundred yards from the restaurant where she'd just had dinner with friends. On the video she had seemed reluctant, but after a couple of minutes, she had climbed into the passenger seat.

Bill Wellings had denied killing her from the moment he was arrested only three days after Diane's death. A trial and an appeal had both found him guilty. Bill's DNA had been found under her fingernails. His fingerprints were matched to numerous partials on her metal belt buckle, and strands of Bill's hair were located under the crown of her Bulova watch. As if that wasn't enough, Bill just happened to drive a forest-green Chevy Malibu.

The evidence was overwhelming but the real clincher came down to motive.

Bill was already on probation for drunkenly accosting then attempting to rape a young woman after she rejected his approaches at a neighbourhood sports bar.

That plus the murder charge was enough to get you the magic needle in the state of Florida.

Peter had been there when his brother first met Diana. Bill got roaring drunk as usual and tried to hit on her while she partied with friends at the next table in a Hawaiian Island-themed restaurant, just off 5th street in Naples, Florida. Wearing his omnipresent fedora, he had continued harassing her until she finally had had enough of his boisterous advances and had the manager throw him out.

In a typical display of his short temper, Bill had thrown his drink over Diana then had staggered out of the restaurant while loudly announcing that she didn't know what she was missing and that she'd regret not hooking up with him.

Peter had rushed to her side and had offered his napkin to help her dry off. There had been something about the innocence of his action and the embarrassed look on his face that Diana found strangely appealing. Before Peter had walked away, she wrote her number on a cocktail napkin and handed it to him.

Peter had made it a point to call her the following day, but she had not answered.

A few hours later, two policemen had appeared at his place of work and had escorted Peter to the Naples police station for questioning. It seemed that his call was the last thing logged on Diana's cell phone account.

Peter had been questioned extensively for the next two days until the police had lost interest in him as the evidence began to pile up against his brother, Bill. Within a matter of days, there was no doubt within the police department or the DA's office as to who had committed the crime.

Bill's drinking and temper had already caused the family so much pain over the years, that with his now being a convicted murderer, Peter felt that it was his family duty to be the one to watch his brother die. Maybe then, everyone could start the process of healing.

There were twelve people in the witness area facing the execution chamber. Most were there in an official capacity, however, in the front row in the last seat on the left, sat the one man that Peter had hoped not to see.

Dan Everett was an ex-Marine and even in his fifties looked as if he could take on a tank single handed.

Diana's father had disliked Peter the from moment they met at Bill's trial. Peter had managed to stay clear of the man, but between the investigation, the trial and the appeals, the two rarely went a week without encountering each other. Dan would openly stare at Peter as if he was to blame for his daughter's death. Rarely did any words pass between the two, but Dan's searing stare said all there was to say.

Even on the day that should have bonded the two closer together, Dan was looking back over his shoulder with clear, smouldering hatred.

Dan only gave up glaring at him when the lights went on within the execution chamber. It was the first chance for the witnesses to see the room. Many gasped as if seeing a magician perform an impossible illusion.

The room was small, about the size of a small office. In the centre was what could almost have been mistaken for a hospital bed were it not for the arm, body and leg restraints.

What had initially spooked the first-time witnesses was how close they were to the death gurney. It almost felt as if, were the glass not there, they could reach from their seats and touch the prisoner.

Peter had seen numerous films that depicted the chamber, but none had captured the stark, utilitarian look of the place. Other than the gurney, there was only a clock and one single, old-fashioned phone mounted to the back wall. It was the most depressing looking space that Peter had ever seen.

After a few minutes, a sombre looking man in a black suit entered the room, wheeling the cart that held the suspended vials that would make up the poison cocktail which would soon end up in Bill's arm. Moments later the prisoner, shackled to two armed guards, was ushered into the room and led to the gurney.

Peter hadn't seen his brother since the last court room hearing and was shocked at what the years had done to him. Bill had always been a big guy. At over six feet, he had weighed in at just under two hundred and twenty pounds prior to the murder. But now, Peter would have been surprised if Bill could tip the scales at one-fifty. His complexion was grey and he looked to have aged twenty years. The brightness of the overhead neon lights caused him to blink and even try unsuccessfully to raise a hand to shield his eyes.

As he was being led to the gurney, Bill spotted Peter through the glass partition. For a moment their eyes locked and Bill pulled against his restraints, clearly screaming something at him. Thankfully the execution chamber was soundproof and the witnesses couldn't hear a thing. Peter watched his brother thrashing at the guards as he continued to yell at the glass partition.

Peter finally turned away and did his best to avoid any further eye contact until Bill was firmly strapped down. Even then, he had trouble looking at his brother, knowing what was about to happen.

At a few minutes to three, the warden stepped over to the wall phone and placed a call to the state governor. Within moments he was advised that there would be no order of clemency and that the execution was to proceed.

Peter couldn't watch as the lethal chemical cocktail was being fed into his brother. The only time he did look up, he saw Bill's chest rise one last time, then lay still.

In a strange show of theatricality, once the doctor confirmed that Bill was dead, a curtain was drawn across the viewing window as if to denote that the entertainment had ended.

Peter was the last person to leave the witness room as he had been advised that, as next of kin, he needed to stay behind to sign some documents before leaving the facility. As Peter watched the other witnesses file out of the room, some looked at him with compassion, a few with uncertainty.

Dan Everett looked at him with pure loathing. "You know what," he seethed, "if you and your brother hadn't taken a shine to my daughter, she'd still be alive."

Peter was about refute the man's words, but realised that what he'd just said was pretty much fact. Maybe Bill was the guilty one, but still, if the two of them hadn't been there that night, Diana would still be among the living.

After ten minutes, a uniformed officer collected Peter and escorted him across the prison grounds to the administration office.

Once seated at a scarred, metal desk, he was given one document at a time by an officious admin assistant with a nametag that read simply 'Hector'. Peter confirmed that he had made arrangements for the body's collection and cremation even though he begrudged every nickel he'd had to spend. His family had flatly refused to cough up even a penny to 'dispose of the killer's corpse', as they put it.

Peter had had no choice but to pay for the cremation himself, though he did choose the cheapest plan he could find. One which included a cardboard coffin, immediate cremation without a service, and the disposition of the ashes. Even that minimalist option ran over six thousand dollars.

The final signature was on a form declaring receipt of personal possessions. It had never dawned on Peter that there would be any property left behind by his brother, but apparently there was.

As each item was transferred from two large Ziploc bags,

the administration assistant checked the item on the list:

Pair of Wrangler jeans, size 40. Used.
Pair of Nike, All-Terrain running shoes, size 12. Used.
Pair of grey, Fruit of the Loom cotton briefs, large. Used.
Black T-shirt with AC/DC logo, size XXL. Used.
Pair of white, calf-length sport socks. Used.
Black, rubber Casio wristwatch. Used.
Nylon Houston Astros jacket, size XXL. Used.
Brown, generic fedora with black band. Used.
Brown, generic wallet. Used.
Pair of gold-rimmed, pilot-style sunglasses. Used
Twenty-eight dollars in bills and eighteen cents in coins.

Once the inventory had been completed and the items were transferred to a plain brown box, the lid was sealed and it was handed over to Peter. Within moments a guard appeared at his side.

"I'll escort you out," he said in a deep baritone.

Once out of the depressing building, he walked back across the campus conspicuously lugging the box of his late brother's possessions. A clear though erroneous assumption to most that he'd just been released from 'the joint'.

Once Peter reached his car, he threw his brother's belongings in the trunk, not wanting the stuff to ride with him up front.

As he was about to get in the driver's seat, a silver Mercedes slowed and stopped next to him. The window slid down and Dan Everett glared out at him.

"Fuck you," he said before raising the window and driving

off.

Peter, his mouth agape, watched as the car left the visitor's lot and pulled onto the main road.

As he got behind the wheel, he decided that though initially vulgar, Dan's words pretty must have summed up all the hatred the man had been feeling for the past few years.

Peter could only hope that the outburst had been somewhat cathartic for him.

Chapter 2
(Present Day)

Peter lay on his back trying to get his heart to slow and his breathing to return to normal.

"That was great," Brenda said as she swung her long, tanned legs out of the king-size bed. "I gotta pee."

Brenda was twenty-five, had natural red hair and a body that was built for speed and stamina.

Peter watched her pert ass as she left the room and wondered how much longer he could deal with the woman's stunted IQ. The problem was that, even though she was basically a 'half-wit', as his mother would have referred to her, she was probably the best lay he'd ever had. What Brenda lacked in intelligence, she made up for in enthusiasm and creativity.

Peter checked his watch and saw that it was almost five o'clock.

"Babe, I gotta run," Peter called to her through the bathroom door.

"Don't go yet. I want more of that beautiful cock of yours."

"Sorry," he shouted back as he pulled on his suit pants. "I have an appointment at five that I can't miss."

The bathroom door opened and Brenda stepped up to

him. She began kissing him roughly as she felt him harden beneath the expensive wool fabric.

"I really have to…" Peter started to say.

Brenda began kissing his neck, then his chest.

"Just one more time?" she cooed.

Her tongue had reached the top of his pants as her hands began undoing his belt.

"What the hell," Peter managed to say just as Breda slid his pants down to his ankles.

Forty-five minutes later, Peter pulled onto Crayton Road just north of central Naples. He drove on for a few hundred yards then turned onto his driveway.

The house was one of the older ones on the street, and though smaller that some of the 'McMansions' that had popped up over the last ten years, his had retained some of the original charm and class of old Naples. It was what the realtors called a ranch style, meaning it was a single storey with a gabled roof.

Inside there were three comfortable bedrooms, a den that he'd converted to an office, and beyond that, a swimming pool. The icing on the cake was that it backed onto an exclusive golf club, giving the impression that their yard just kept on going right across the manicured fairway.

When he opened the front door, he could smell freshly baked cookies.

"I'm home," he called out. "I'm gonna jump in the shower."

"The cookies will be cool enough to eat in about ten minutes."

Genna Wellings, his wife of over fifteen years, appeared

from the kitchen. Her hands were concealed within oven gloves made to look like Lobster claws. She was petite, blonde and despite producing two boys, had managed to keep her figure close to the original design specs.

"That'll work for me," Peter replied as he headed down the hallway to the master bedroom.

"Don't I get a kiss?" Genna asked.

"I'm all sweaty. You wouldn't enjoy it."

Genna rolled her eyes wondering why he always insisted on driving his classic 911 with the top down. Even without the summer humidity, ninety degrees while stuck in rush hour traffic was still intense.

She walked over to the sliding door that lead to the patio and was met with the sound of their two sons screaming maniacally as they cannon-balled into the pool.

"There'll be cookies ready in about ten minutes. Why don't you guys get out and dry off?"

"Can't we have them out here?"

"You've had enough sun for today. Come inside and cool off."

Despite the exaggerated moaning from the pair, she knew they'd get out almost as soon as her back was turned. Her macadamia nut and white chocolate chip cookies were that good.

Once he'd finished showering, Peter returned to their kitchen/diner. The first thing he saw were the twins, Mike and Greg. At seven years old, they were both big for their age. While not strictly identical, they were still very alike. The only real difference was that Mike had sandy blond hair like Genna, and Greg had dark hair like Peter.

As soon as the boys saw their father, they began talking excitedly, both at the same time.

"Did you hear tha-" Mike started.

"-it's going to snow tonight," Greg finished.

"Our teacher told us that it's going to be like a buzzard!" Mike stated.

"Blizzard, you dork," Greg corrected him, giggling.

"He said we might even get enough to make a snowman," Mike added.

"Have they told you the exciting news?" Genna said as she appeared from the laundry room.

"Yes, they have," Peter replied. "Though I hate to be the one to tell you guys, but it has never snowed in Naples … ever!"

"We know that," Greg said, indignantly. "This will be the first time ever."

"It's all cause of mobile warming!" Mike advised.

Greg did an exaggerated facepalm.

"I think you mean global warming," Genna suggested, trying to keep from laughing.

"Double dork," Greg said.

"Dad, if it does snow and we get to make a snowman, can we get some stuff from the attic so we can dress him up?"

Peter looked to Genna to gauge her feelings on the subject. All she offered was a shrug.

"Okay," he replied. "You can go through the boxes marked *Grandad*. I'm not sure there's anything that exciting, but if you find something, you can use it. However, when no snow turns up, I want you to put the stuff right back where you found it."

"Yay!" the boys squealed in unison.

"You know," Genna said, "the local station said it was definitely going to snow."

"If, and it's a big if, it does actually snow, we're way too far south to get any real accumulation. If anything it'll be a light dusting."

"If you say so," she replied. "Why don't we let them have a rummage tonight, that way there won't be a mad panic in the morning."

"Can we bring the boxes to our room?" Greg asked.

"They're kind of dusty. Maybe..." Genna started to say.

"Sure," Peter interrupted. "That sounds like a good idea."

"Who wants cookies first?" Genna asked trying not to show her annoyance.

While the boys were scarfing down their cookies, Genna reached across the table and took hold of Peter's hand.

"Maybe a little snow might be good distraction tomorrow. I know how much you hate the anniversary."

"I don't hate it," he said with a forced smile. "I just hate to be reminded about it."

"I can't imagine what it must have been like being there, watching your own brother ..."

"Then don't," Peter said flatly as he pulled his hand away. He then grabbed a couple of cookies and stormed off to the garage so he could lower the spring-loaded ladder that led to the attic.

The boys loved being given unsupervised access to the space above the garage. It was a place of mystery, wonder and imagination. Forts could be built, haunted corners investigated, and on occasion, treasures found.

After some goofing off, they carried the two boxes marked *Grandad* downstairs. They were heavy, but the two made good time lowering them to the garage floor then transporting them to their bedroom.

Once behind closed doors they rummaged through the water-stained boxes and were immediately disappointed at the contents. There was nothing they could dress a snowman in. What they found instead were old letters, cheap-looking mementos and a couple of pee-stained long johns that neither of them wanted to touch.

"This is all crap," Mike said.

"It's worse than crap," Greg replied. "It's the crap that crappy crap craps!"

Mike had heard the line a hundred times, but it still made him giggle.

"So what are we going to put on the snowman?" Mike asked.

Greg made a big show of checking that the door was closed and they were alone in the room.

"I don't know if you noticed, but at the very back there was another box just like these."

"Was it labelled *Grandad*?"

Greg shook his head. "It didn't have any writing on it at all, but it looked old."

"We were told that we could only use the *Grandad* boxes," Mike reminded him.

"I don't think they even know it's up there. It's covered in dust and stuff and doesn't look like it's ever been opened."

"Maybe we should ask," Mike suggested.

"If we ask, they might say no. If we don't ask, we can always say that we thought it was one of the *Grandad* boxes."

Mike gave it a moment's thought then finally nodded his head.

They both snuck back up into the loft expecting the box to need both of them to carry it back downstairs. It didn't. In fact it was disappointingly light. Greg carried it all by himself and once they had it back in their room, they crossed their fingers and tore off the brown, curled tape.

As they pealed open the brittle cardboard, the smell of mildew and old sweat rose into the air.

"Yuck," Mike said as he squeezed his nostrils closed.

Greg wasn't as bothered by the smell and simply emptied the contents onto the floor.

"Wow," he said while prodding the small pile with his right foot. "This is exactly what we wanted."

Mike knelt down and, covering his hand with his sleeve, pushed the items apart so they could get a better look.

"Who do you think this stuff belongs to?" he asked.

"I don't know but it's in our attic, so I guess it means it's Mom's or Dad's."

"This doesn't look like anything they'd ever wear."

"Not now, but don't forget, they're really old. Maybe they used to wear stuff like this."

Mike used his foot to separate out one particular item. It was a faded, black t-shirt with the letters AC and DC separated by a red lightning bolt.

"I don't know," Greg said waiting for Mike to look up and see what he was wearing.

Mike finally looked over at his brother and burst out laughing. He had put on a pair of giant, gold-framed sunglasses and a funny looking hat that was a million sizes too big for him.

"How do I look?"

Chapter 3

Genna knocked on the converted den door and stepped inside, expecting to see her husband sitting in front of the double monitors on his desk. Instead, he was looking at his iPhone screen.

Peter immediately ended the call as casually as he could, pretending that the conversation had reached its natural conclusion. It might have worked if his pants hadn't been pulled down around his ankles, and his erection, though diminishing, was still plainly evident.

"Jesus Christ, Peter. It's bad enough that you feel the need to cheat on me, but do you have to have phone sex in our home?"

Genna could almost hear Peter's brain whirring away, trying desperately to find some excuse for his current situation.

"I was just getting undressed so I could put on my sweats," he mumbled.

"That explains the boner, then," Genna shot back.

For a moment, Peter tried to decide what response options he had, then chose the worst one believing that offence was the best defence and went on the attack.

"Yeah well if you didn't barge into my room uninvited…" he said lamely as he stood and pulled up his pants.

"It doesn't matter if I came in or not, you were still playing with yourself while talking, I assume, to your latest concubine."

"Concubine?" Peter shot back. "Who the hell uses that word?"

"Would you prefer whore?"

"I'd prefer you stopped jumping to conclusions."

"I found you on the phone with your pants on the floor and your cock in your hand. Please. What other conclusion could I have jumped to?"

"There's no one else. I just like porn."

"So there's no mistress?" Genna asked, feigning hope.

"Of course not. I wouldn't do that to you."

"That's a relief," Genna said. "Because when someone called Brenda texted you while you were in the shower, and said that you'd forgotten your wallet at her place, I was kind of concerned."

"Brenda's a ... new paralegal in the office. I drove her home so we could go over a complicated case that was coming up."

"Sure," Genna replied. "However, there's still the problem of you walking into the house earlier this evening smelling like eau de vagina, plus Brenda did happen to add one last thought in her text."

Peter stared defiantly back at her.

"Shall I say what she wrote?" she asked.

Peter didn't answer. He remembered full well what the text had said.

"She said that she loves having your balls in her mouth. I must say. She sounds like a lovely girl."

"What do you want me to say?" he asked.

"There's nothing you can say. I'm leaving you."

"Listen..."

He was interrupted by Greg and Mike charging into the room.

"It's snowing!" they shouted in unison.

Peter stepped to the office window and opened the blinds. It was dark out, but by the illumination from the room and the back yard lights, he could see that it was indeed snowing. He stared in amazement, watching the Dorito-sized snowflakes eddy and swirl on the way to the ground.

The four walked to the living room where they had an unobstructed view of the yard. It wasn't just snowing, it was settling.

"Can we build the snowman? Greg asked.

"Please?" Mike added.

Peter didn't know how to answer.

"Let's wait till the morning then I can help you," Genna said.

"But it might be all gone by then," Mike pleaded.

Genna took another look outside and shook her head. She couldn't tell where their patio ended and the lawn began. She guessed there was already a good three inches of snow on the ground.

"It won't be gone," she replied. "I promise. Why don't you get the stuff ready so we can decorate the snowman first thing in the morning."

The two boys looked happy at the compromise and charged down the hall, back to their bedroom.

"I thought you were leaving?"

"Not in the middle of a blizzard," she advised.

Genna finished tidying up the kitchen and started the dishwasher. She turned on the TV and tuned in to the local Fort Myers station. They had interrupted scheduled programming to bring their viewers the unprecedented breaking news: Southwestern Florida was under a blizzard warning for the first time in recorded history.

There followed dozens of local reporters, all insufficiently dressed for the occasion, standing at notable locations throughout the area, all being prodigiously snowed upon. Genna marvelled at how beautiful the night shots of palm trees, golf courses and beaches looked under a fresh blanket of snow.

She momentarily forgot the pain and anger she'd been feeling until she noticed their gilded drink cart that sat at the end of the room.

The bottle of Courvoisier was gone as was Peter's favourite snifter. He'd obviously grabbed the brandy while she was in the kitchen and planned to deal with this latest life crisis in his usual way.

If history was anything to go by, he'd pass out on his fold-out bed and not appear until late morning.

Chapter 4

Genna had been right; the snow may have stopped at some point in the night, but there was plenty left in their front yard to build a substantial snowman. Mike and Greg were already dressed as warmly as possible considering they had no serious winter wear and were begging to be released out into their newfound, white wonderland.

Genna wanted their father to be part of what would almost certainly be an indelible memory, but he had spent the night in his home-office and would not respond to her knocking. She tried numerous times but, on the last occasion when she pressed her ear against the door, she could hear the distinct sound of deep snoring.

She knew from many similar mornings that the door wasn't locked. Genna could simply open it and try to rouse him, however, that was definitely not the safer option. When Peter regained consciousness after a major bender, he was meaner than usual. The sort of mean that would lead to her ending up in the emergency room lying about walking into a door or slipping in the bathroom.

No. If the door was closed, the door would stay closed until he felt it was time to emerge.

Even though his not being there for the kids was tragic, with the roads already cleared and the schools open for all who could attend, time for building a snowman was fast running out. Resigned and cursing Peter under her breath, she opened the front door and let Mike and Greg out onto their small, snow covered front lawn.

Each boy carried a supermarket shopping bag filled with what they had looted from the attic the previous evening. Once outside, they stared at the white blanket that covered most of the neighbourhood.

Having never seen snow before in their lives, they weren't exactly sure what to do. In a frantic effort to get the boys immersed in the fun of snow-based construction while still protecting them from frostbite, she ran inside and grabbed a box of heavy duty freezer bags. After double-gloving them both, she showed them how to make snowballs.

Despite the protection the plastic bags offered, most of their manual dexterity was severely restricted. After a very brief snowball battle, Genna suggested they focus what time was left on making the snowman.

This proved much harder than she had expected – there just wasn't enough snow to roll 3 balls into sufficient size for the base, body and head. Instead, she ended up using their rake and scraped all the snow into one central area. From there, the three were able to create a four foot tall mound, pack it as hard as they could, then remove the snow from the waste and neck areas.

Genna glanced at her watch. "Okay. We've got five minutes to decorate it. This is what we are going to do…"

She had the boys empty everything out of the bags. She then chose what items could be used and which couldn't, such as the AC/DC T-shirt because of the difficulty with trying to pull it over the top of the snow pile.

Together they managed to put the Houston Astros jacket onto the middle orb and the sneakers were tucked under the base as if it were his feet.

"We're going to need a few more things," Genna announced as she sprinted into the house. "Don't do anything for a second."

She grabbed a drooping carrot from the chiller drawer and a bag of coffee beans from the countertop.

Once back outside, she helped the boys insert the carrot mid-head, then had them use the beans to fashion the outline of a mouth. Once that task was completed, the pair of gold-rimmed pilot's sunglasses were fitted just above the carrot. The finishing touch was to gently place the worn fedora on top of the head.

The three stepped back and examined their work.

"Not bad," Genna said, nodding.

"It doesn't look like the snowmen I've seen on TV," Gregg whined.

"No it doesn't," Genna replied. "Ours is way better. Grandad's clothes look great."

Both boys looked at each other with guilty expressions.

"Actually ... we found another box in the attic," Mike confessed. "This all came from there."

"No worries, come on — it's time to go," Genna announced, having not even listened to what Mike had said. "You two stand in front of it so I can take a picture."

The two posed, pulling their usual goofy photo expression. Once she'd taken a few shots, she bundled them into the pre-loaded car and after carefully driving across their unploughed semi-circle driveway, she gently accelerated wondering if she'd have time to swing back to the house before heading to her office so that she could make sure that Peter didn't miss work.

After doing a quick mental calculation she realised that there was no way she could make it back to the house and not end up late herself.

For a brief moment she started to stress about how angry Peter would be and that he would doubtless blame his oversleeping on her rather than the brandy.

"To hell with him," she whispered to herself so the boys couldn't hear.

Chapter 5

Peter was scared to open his eyes. Even in his sleep he'd felt the throbbing headache growing into something nuclear. He tried to sense where exactly the pain was centred in his head, but realised that it wasn't in any one place. It was gnawing at his sinuses, thumping at his temples and stabbing at the back of his skull.

He managed to open one eye, and even in the dark afforded by the black-out curtains, he could just make out the bottle of Courvoisier siting on the table. What he saw went a long way to explaining the state of his head.

The bottle was empty.

Peter tried to remember how much had been in it at the start of the evening, but the tangle of black foil from the top of the bottle told the entire story. He'd opened it last night and had managed to drink the whole thing.

Just the thought of having consumed that much brandy flooded him with a new wave of nausea.

He shut the one opened eye and tried to find a way back into sleep. He knew that work was out of the question and that the only thing that was going to put any sort of dent into his headache was a few more hours of recuperative z's.

The problem was that he needed to piss. Downing a bottle of brandy was going to require some serious waste disposal.

He tried to sit up but the change in pressure within his head caused bolts of jagged pain to ricochet around within his cranium.

Peter collapsed back onto the fold-out bed and closed both eyes until the pain diminished. As bad as it was, the urge to urinate was worse.

Peter managed to roll himself off the bed and literally crawl across the darkened den to the en-suite shower room. He was afraid that turning the light on would result in still more pain so he felt his way to the toilet and somehow managed to raise himself to a sitting position.

Starting the process took a surprisingly long time and even when his bladder began to release its contents, the stream was weak.

When Peter felt he'd given back enough liquid, he tried to stand with limited success. The pain doubled and he was again forced down on his hands and knees for the return journey to the bed.

As he made his way across the Berber carpet he felt wetness on his knees and the bottom of his hands. He raised one palm to his nose and sniffed, worried that maybe at some point during the night he'd pissed himself on the way to the toilet.

The liquid held no odour.

Peter made it to the bed and crawled back on top. He tried to lay quietly to still the throbbing in his head, but he suddenly felt cold.

Really cold.

He pulled the thin blanket all the way up to his chin but it did little good. In fact, if anything, it got colder still.

Just as he felt that sleep was about to take him away regardless of the temperature, he felt a drop of icy water land on his nose.

Peter decided it must have been a mini hallucination.

Then another drop landed on his forehead. That time he knew what he'd felt: a very cold drip of water. A terrifying thought jumped into his head – the snow. What if it really had snowed heavily and the roof was being damaged by its accumulated weight? After all, Floridian rooves were not designed for such weather.

Peter fumbled for the light cord on the side table, but couldn't seem to find it. Finally, he located the plastic switch and the light snapped on with such intense brightness that he had to keep his eyes shut tightly until he could ease them both open, one millimetre at a time.

Peter's vision was blurry, but for a split second he thought that his long dead brother was standing next to the bed. It was the jacket, the sunglasses and the fedora that did it. It was a natural mistake, except for the fact that he'd watched his brother die years earlier.

Peter realised that what he was looking at was only a snowman that for some reason seemed to be wearing his brother's clothing. It took a good few moments for Peter to put some of the pieces together. The boys were going to build a snowman that morning. He'd obviously not been capable of helping so someone, probably his bitch of a wife, thought it would be funny to build it in his office while he was passed out.

As for the clothes, they had been buried somewhere in

the attic, so the boys probably found them and, not realising what they were, thought they'd put them on the damn snowman.

He could just imagine the pair of them giggling as they carried in the piles of snow. They probably thought it was funny and that Daddy would appreciate their humour.

The problem was, Daddy wasn't in the mood for any humour and the snowman was now melting on his fifty-dollar-a-square-yard carpet.

"You little shits," Peter whispered. "I'll show you how funny I think you are. You too, Genna. Maybe I'll just destroy some of your shit while you're gone. Better still, maybe all three of you need a little refresher course in respect. Maybe when you all get home I'll have my favourite belt ready so I can really show you how I feel about your little surp…"

"Oh my god, will you shut the fuck up," a voice cut him off.

Peter looked up in shock. Did the voice really come from the snowman? His mind having been jolted back into some sort of focus, he stared in disbelief at his brother's jacket, glasses and most especially, his hat.

"Surprised to see me, little brother?"

Though Peter clearly heard the voice, *his brother's voice*, the weird coffee bean mouth never moved. Then again, why would it? It was pretty obvious that he was having some sort of crazed hallucination; at least that's what he hoped was happening.

"You're not real," he said in barely a whisper.

"Not real? How can you say that? Did you really think I'd never come back? We need to talk about what you did."

Peter looked away. "You are not real. I just drank too much."

"There's no question you drank too much, then again, you always did. But as far as not being real, I'm kinda offended. I mean, I know I died and all, but don't you even recognise me just a little bit?"

Peter laughed to himself.

"What's so funny, Peter?"

"You asking if I recognise you. I mean, come on. You're a fucking snowman."

Peter jumped when the snowman's headed nodded as if agreeing.

"You make a good point, Pete. Maybe this will help."

As Peter looked on in horror, a snow arm rose from the white torso. An icy hand formed at its end and grabbed hold of the gold-rimmed sunglasses. It lifted them off the carrot at which point the arm lowered back down and together with the glasses, melded back with the rest of the snow.

"Look up, Peter."

Peter didn't want to look up. It was becoming obvious that whatever the intent of the thing standing in his office, it wasn't there to make friends.

"I said look up," the voice demanded.

He looked back up at the head and saw that with the glasses removed, a pair of very human eyes were looking back at him.

"I always thought it was funny that everyone in the family had blue eyes except me," his brother's voice said.

Peter stared at the hazel eyes and knew without a doubt whom they belonged to. The unique black triangle at the very bottom of the right iris was clear as day.

"This isn't possible," Peter gasped.

"Anything's possible if you want it badly enough. Isn't that true, little brother? For instance, you must have really wanted that girl in the restaurant. I mean, to steal my car so you could pick her up and then kill her … wow. That's some serious shit. Killing her was bad enough, but framing me — your brother! That still haunts me and I've been dead for fifteen years."

Peter just stared into his brother's eyes.

"What do you have to say for yourself?"

"There's nothing to say," Peter replied, turning away from the accusing, hazel eyes.

"Not even that you're sorry?" Bill's voice suggested. "I mean, that would at least be a good starting point, don't you think?"

"I don't need to say anything." Peter's voice had turned menacing and cold. "I mean, yeah, you're here and all, but what exactly do you think you can do to me? Look at you. You're literally melting right in front of me. All I have to do is watch as the problem goes away all by itself."

"That's the thing with you, Pete. You never gave me any credit for anything. Well that's not true, I guess. You sure gave me the credit for killing that nice girl, but other than that, you always thought I was some sort of idiot."

"You still are," Peter replied. "You think you're threatening, but you're just a mound of frozen water. In fact. I'm going to end this right now."

Peter got to his feet and staggered into the shower room. He emerged moments later with an electric hairdryer in his hand. He plugged it in to a socket in the base of the lamp them turned it on to high.

"Now I get to watch my problems literally melt away," Peter mocked as he pointed the dryer directly at the snowman.

Chapter 6

Genna sat in the back of a police car, the door open, waiting to be told that she could finally re-enter her home. Minutes earlier, two officers from the coroner's office had wheeled out a black body bag. Inside it was the lifeless corpse of her late husband. The body she'd found when she decided at the last minute to come home for lunch, something she never did.

As the men shut the back of their van, one of the officers walked over to her. Genna stood to greet him. He looked too young to be tasked with such a serious duty.

"Mrs Wellings, we've removed your husband from the house."

Though said with a note of sympathy, Genna could tell by the ease with which the words flowed that he'd said the same thing with minor variances hundreds, if not thousands, of times before.

"Thank you," she replied. "Do you still think it was an accident?"

"I have no doubt. He was standing on a soaking wet carpet when he dropped the hairdryer. We're not sure where the water originated, but there'll be a forensic building inspector here later today who will determine where it came from."

"Any guesses?" Genna asked.

"If I had to throw my two cents in, I'd say that snowfall last night had something to with it. All that extra weight on the roof pushing liquid beneath it as it melted. The water could have found a way through some flashing or even under the eaves. Once inside it could have travelled any number of ways to end up in that room."

Genna nodded even though she was too exhausted to fully understand what the man had said.

"Can I go inside yet?" she asked.

"Unfortunately, that won't be possible until the building inspector has been and gone," he replied. "Do you have somewhere else you can go?"

"My folks live in Pelican Bay. I guess I can camp there with my kids for a while."

The officer sighed. "I assume they don't know yet," he said, showing official concern.

"No they don't. I was going to take them out of school early, but decided that there wasn't much point. Might as well let them have a little more normalcy in their lives before I drop the hammer."

The officer nodded, looking concerned. Genna knew he would have seen the fold-out bed and the brandy bottle, probably empty. He clearly felt that a few extra words of kindness were called for.

"You know what they say, when God shuts a door, he opens a window."

Even though she thought it a strange thing for a police officer to say, Genna appreciated the sentiment. For a moment she wondered if he'd perceived the fact that she wasn't even remotely sad about Peter being gone.

"May I at least pick up what's left of the snowman decorations?" she asked pointing to the front lawn.

The officer smiled. "You know, when we first arrived, everyone was having a heck of a time working out what those items were doing out on your lawn. The responding officers even wondered if they were connected to what happened to your husband. Thankfully a couple of your neighbours had taken pictures of the snowman before it melted so the mystery was solved.

Genna forced a smile.

"When do you think you will be releasing the body?" she asked. "I need to start thinking about the funeral."

"I can't say for certain as there's quite a number of cases before your husband."

"Cases?"

"Autopsies."

"I thought you said it was clearly an accident."

"The immediate cause of death isn't in doubt. Why he dropped the hairdryer in the first place still is."

"Does it really matter?" she asked.

"To the state it does. If he dropped it because of some terminal health emergency, like a heart attack or stroke, his death would no longer necessarily be recorded as accidental."

"I see," Genna replied.

"There is one thing that has us a little puzzled," the officer said. "Did your husband eat a lot of ice cream or frozen drinks?"

"No. Why?"

"His throat and mouth had what appeared to be extensive freezer burn."

"Like on a piece of chicken?" Genna asked then immediately regretted her words. "That sounded bad. I'm sorry."

"Nothing to apologise for. And, yes, very like what you'd see on a piece of poultry that's been in the freezer too long."

"He didn't like cold drinks," Genna replied. "What else could cause it?"

"Never seen anything quite like it personally, but at a seminar last year in Chicago, they showed photos of similar damage caused to bodies that had suffocated after being trapped within avalanches."

"I somehow doubt that was the cause here. That would be impossible, wouldn't it?"

"I would have said that snow in Southern Florida was impossible until last night."

"Sort of like a snowball's chance in hell?" Genna asked, immediately regretting her flippant choice of words.

On her way to pick up the boys, Genna stopped at the Salvation Army thrift shop on Tamiami Trail. The jacket had almost completely dried, but the fedora was still a little damp. She considered keeping the sunglasses for the kids but decided that any part of the snowman would just remind her of last night and Peter.

"I don't know if you will even want these things, but it didn't feel right just throwing them away," Genna said to the overweight woman behind the counter.

The volunteer lifted the jacket out of the box and after a

brief inspection, placed it on the glass countertop. She then did the same with the Fedora.

"Mind if I have a look at those, Martha?" a voice said from behind one of the carousel clothing racks.

As Genna turned, a man stepped up to the counter. He was older, unshaven and scruffy.

"Tom, you know you have to wait until we stock an item before you can have it," the woman scolded before turning to Genna. "Tom here treats this place like his own personal clothing rack."

Martha gave him a shake of the head then handed him the jacket. He practically grabbed it out of her hand then put it on.

"Can I try on the hat as well?" Tom reached over and took it off the counter then he placed it on his head and beamed. "How do I look?"

Genna was about to say that he looked just fine, then realised that he looked more than just that. He somehow looked cleaner and healthier than he had only a few moments earlier.

Martha reached into the box and held out the gold rimmed sunglasses.

"You might as well have the complete set," Martha said.

Tom took them from her with surprising care and put them on.

"I'm lovin' the way I feel dressed in this stuff," Tom stated as he glanced at himself in a full length mirror attached to a square pillar.

"You look pretty good," Martha said with honest sincerity.

"I feel great," Tom said as he adjusted the fedora so that it rested just a little more forward on his head.

"You know, Martha, I don't get my welfare money this early in the week, any chance I can owe you?"

Martha looked from Tom to Genna then back again.

"Oh heck. As I haven't even logged them in yet, if this kind woman was to simply give them to you, there's not much I could do about it."

Tom looked hopefully at Genna.

"They're all yours," she announced, happy that she'd managed to give someone a little pleasure on that day.

"Thank you kindly, ma'am." Tom removed the glasses and gave her a big wink.

Genna smiled back and looked into his hazel eyes, one of which now had a black triangle in the lower half of the iris. For some reason, she suddenly felt uncomfortable and chilled.

"I gotta say," Tom continued, putting the glasses back on, "this little outfit makes me feel like a whole new man."

LONG SHADOWS

Chapter 1

When Jason Wild received the invitation, he at first thought that there'd been some sort of mistake. Even though his writing had started to take off, and his latest novel was number four on the New York Times bestseller list, he felt the invite couldn't possibly have been for him.

He re-read the gilt-trimmed piece of stationery and confirmed that it most definitely was his name at the top. Even with that unequivocal proof, Jason still couldn't understand why he had been invited to the attend the annual Dark Hearts Dinner.

He'd of course heard of it, but the extraordinarily exclusive function only ever included the elite of the horror writing world. While Jason was a horror writer, he at no point ever felt that he'd reached the level of authors like Stephen King and Graham Masterton.

Yet, here was the invitation. The location was not given. It never was until a few days prior, though the nearest airport was divulged so that travel could at least be booked.

Each year a site was chosen based entirely on atmosphere and its documented history of hauntings.

Every fibre in Jason's body was screaming for him to tell everyone he knew that he'd just scored an invite to one of the most infamous dinners in the world. The problem was, none of the invitees or the hotel staff were permitted to divulge any details of the event prior to it taking place. Failure to follow the secrecy mandate would result in a lifetime ban from not just the dinners, but all other gatherings that randomly took place around the globe.

The most closely guarded secret was what was actually said at the dinners. No word spoken at the event was ever to be divulged.

As astonishing as it seemed, no one had ever broken the bond of secrecy. After each soirée, the location always leaked out as did the menu and even the names of the attendees, but never even a hint as to what was discussed ever found its way into the public domain.

The only clue as to the location was a small note at the bottom of the invite that simply said: 'Where, sadly, one of our own, who recently passed, based her batty stories, lived her life and where in this lowly city her legacy shall last.'

Though certainly cryptic, Jason knew the answer immediately. He especially liked the part about the 'lowly city'. It was obvious to him that the author who recently passed was Anne Rice. She wrote about vampires and lived mainly in New Orleans. The lowly comment was not meant as a slight against the city, rather the fact that it lies below sea level, protected only by a series of levies.

Jason booked his flight for the day prior to the dinner. The invitation mentioned fine company, exquisite food and grand accommodations. He hoped that the organisers were not just reserving the room for one single night otherwise, as he wanted to get there a full day ahead of the event, he was going to have a mad scramble to find a bed once they revealed the actual location and disclosed the accommodation details.

Jason had a thousand questions but had no way of getting them answered. He checked the invite carefully, hoping there would be a contact number or even an email address, but there was nothing. As a last hope, he checked the envelope just in case there was some clue as to the sender's identity, but instead of providing a hint, it just added to the mystery.

The envelope held his name and address and looked to have been handwritten in a fine, italic font. There was nothing else on either the back or the front of the cream coloured paper; not even a stamp.

Jason stared at it wondering how the hell it had ever reached him without having gone through the postal service. He couldn't imagine anyone hand delivering every invite, but then again, it was a gathering of folk who had spent their lives writing about the darker side of the macabre and paranormal. Finding a creepy way to deliver the invite would have been child's play.

The days dragged by, but no further communication came through the mail. After two weeks, Jason started wondering if he had been pranked. His best friend, Harlich Cox, was known for his practical jokes and something like a fake invite would be just the sort of trick he'd play on a friend.

Days passed and he gave up on the invite being genuine. Jason pulled his Mini Cooper S into his subterranean parking space and started to plan a suitable revenge gag to get back at his friend. He walked up the dreary concrete staircase to the second floor, then made his way down an open walkway that faced his complex's minuscule pool. He stopped for a second to watch his neighbour, Miranda, as she swam with strong purposeful strokes.

She was gorgeous and would have raised the heart rate of just about any straight man as she moved through the water with aquatic grace.

"Don't waste your time," Doug Collis said as he walked by. "She's not into men," he continued in a conspiratorial whisper before making for the stairs.

Doug was in his forties, had a pear-shaped body and lived in the last unit at the far end of the walkway. He was one of the few straight residents in the West Hollywood condo complex and considered himself to be something of a ladies' man. Jason had seen the never-ending stream of women that frequented Doug's unit and was stunned at how dreadfully drab they all were. It was almost as if poor Dougie was aiming for quantity instead of quality.

For some reason, Doug always felt the need to make some sort of misogynistic comment to him every time they ran into each other. Jason played along. He had to. His books were starting to sell and his agent had strongly suggested that he not come out just yet.

"Success can be a fragile mistress," Art had said on numerous occasions. "You write dark horror stories and your demographic is straight males between twenty-five and fifty. Don't give them a reason to turn on you. Once you're selling millions of copies, you can revisit the idea, but until then, be dark, moody and straight."

Not for the first time, he mulled over that conversation sullenly as he walked towards his front door.

He inserted the key, twisted it and then pushed the door open.

He switched on the light and saw a dead man swinging from his ceiling fan.

Chapter 2

It took Jason a few seconds to realise that it wasn't a dead man at all. It was a life-size, cardboard cut-out of a purple-faced man in a blue suit that was designed to look like a dead body. As he approached it, Jason could see that there was an embossed envelope taped to one side.

He couldn't fathom how this had ended up in his home and for a brief moment wondered if Harlich had played some part in the subterfuge. Once he'd opened the envelope and read the contents however, he knew that his friend could not possibly be the culprit. The plain piece of rice paper that was tucked inside gave the final details for the Dark Hearts Dinner.

There was no way the organisers would have trusted any of their secrets to someone like Harlich. He was the person to go to if you wanted a piece of information to go viral on social media. If secrecy was critical, he would be the last possible choice.

The dinner was to take place in five days' time in the ballroom of the Bourbon Orleans Hotel. The ballroom was said to be the most haunted room in the city's most haunted hotel. The evening would start with cocktails at eight o'clock with the dinner itself starting one hour later. Attire was to be formal, with men wearing a red bow tie and women a red scarf.

The note also said that Jason's hotel room had been prebooked for three nights with the dinner being held on the middle one.

The final words on the flimsy material read: PLEASE EAT ME AFTER READING.

Jason did as instructed and was surprised to find that the paper dissolved in his mouth, leaving behind a subtle taste of mint chocolate.

The flight to New Orleans was uneventful though Jason did notice Dean Koontz making for the first class section of the plane. Being on a tighter budget, Jason was relegated to the rear of the aircraft. He was dying to sneak up front and introduce himself, but realised that he was almost certainly going to be dining with Koontz the very next day and meeting him then would be reward enough.

Along with Stephen King, Dean Koontz was one of Jason's horror writing favourites. His book *Watchers* had inspired Jason to write his first short story.

Once the plane landed, Jason had planned to head towards the taxi queue when he noticed a woman who was the spitting image of Elvira, Mistress of the Dark holding up a white sign with Jason's name on it.

He was so stunned at both the theatrics and the thoughtfulness of the organisers that he at first didn't notice a number of other Elvira lookalikes waiting to pick up their designated charges.

Once Jason had identified himself, Elvira grabbed his carry-on bag and led him out of the terminal. While he loved the idea of the guests being picked up by such an iconic figure, he was a little freaked out at the fact that she never said a word to him.

Jason tried to start up a conversation on the walk from the arrivals terminal to the parking area, but the woman seemed to not even be aware that he had spoken. His sense of discomfort was doubled when they reached her vehicle. It was a 1960's era hearse. The area in the back where the coffin would have rested had been transformed into a U-shaped seating area.

"I don't suppose you plan on explaining any of this do you?" Jason asked her as she held the door open for him.

She ignored him completely.

As soon as they left the parking area, the hearse was filled with what sounded like the background score to any number of classic Hammer horror films.

The trip took just over fifty minutes due to heavy traffic as they approached the Quarter. The hotel was tucked away on Orleans Street just off Bourbon Street. The two-hundred-year-old building was the epitome of New Orleans grandeur, style and grace.

Jason thanked the driver and attempted to give her a tip, but she stared right through to his soul, turned away, then slid back into her hearse. He looked to the doorman to see if he thought her behaviour was unusual, but the man just shrugged as if such goings-on were pretty much the norm in the crescent city.

When Jason got to his room he was initially surprised to see how normal it looked considering the hotel's haunted reputation. The décor was old-world elegant. A four-poster bed sat atop a huge Persian rug. The wall at the head of the bed was painted a deep, blood red, yet even that didn't seem out of place.

What did, however, was the bunch of flowers in a crystal vase that was positioned on a small writing desk. A dozen perfect black roses. He hadn't even known that such a thing existed. He approached the blooms and saw that when looked at from above, one red rose was visible in the centre of the bunch.

He couldn't help thinking that it looked like some sort of wound.

A card lay next to the vase. It read simply: 'Welcome to the club.'

Jason spent a couple of hours roaming the French Quarter. There was something about the feel of New Orleans that always gave him a slight case of the creeps. Its history, steeped in piracy, slavery and dark beliefs, was almost tangibly present wherever you walked within the city.

When Jason returned to his room, a red envelope had been pushed under his door. In it was a cream-coloured piece of card with a handwritten message.

'Join me at the Belle Epoque Absinthe Lounge at 7:00.'

Below the invite were the initials T.H. Jason felt a chill of excitement filter through his body. While the initials T.H. wouldn't normally have any great meaning, considering where he was and the purpose of his visit, the initials could well belong to his writing idol, Tim Hall.

Hall was the de facto king of the horror genre. His book, *Feelers,* even thirty years after its publication, was still on the New York Times best seller list. Of course, it was also possible that one of the organisers with the same initials was behind the invite, but Jason chose to hope for the best.

Jason changed into a new pair of black jeans, a white silk shirt and a black waistcoat. It wasn't his usual look, but considering where he was and why he was there, a little creativity in apparel seemed the right way to go.

The lounge was a short walk from the hotel. A severe looking doorman/bouncer gave Jason a quick glare, then smiled.

"Welcome, Mister Wild. Your party is already here."

Jason had no idea how the man knew who he was, but the moment he stepped inside, the hostess gave him almost the identical greeting before asking him to follow her. The main room was darkly lit, shabby-chic and had a distinct old-world feel.

As they approached the back of an olive green, leather sofa a man rose to his feet and slowly turned. Jason almost gasped. He was older and frailer than he expected, but there was no doubt as to his identity. Tim Hall gave the hostess an acknowledging nod then held out his hand.

"I've heard you referred to as the new Tim Hall," he said with a smile. "If you are the new me, I felt we should at least get to know each other."

Jason had a moment of panic when he thought that he wasn't going to be able to form words. Shaking hands with one of the world's most prolific and extraordinarily talented writers was beyond surreal.

"It's an honour," Jason managed to say without it sounding too gushing.

"Being an honour makes me sound way too lofty. We're

just a couple of writers getting together to knock back a few cold ones."

The two sat facing each other and for a brief moment, Tim openly studied Jason.

"You're young," he commented. "I hate you a little for that."

"You were younger than me when your first book went to number one."

"That's true, but after reading a couple of yours, I have to agree with the critics. Your style and mine are very similar, but you are able to write to this generation. Try as I might, my prose is getting a little dated."

"I don't agree. Horror is timeless and your style fits the format better than anyone else on the planet," Jason said.

"You're not including yours?"

"Especially not mine. I have a long way to go before I can write with the same confidence that you have."

"That's very kind of you to say so, but as I said, I've read some of your work. You seem to enjoy the slow build up, just as I do."

"That's the way I want a story to unfold," Jason said. "Some of the new horror writers start turning up the heat in the first few pages. I like the reader to not even realise what's happening until it's too late."

"Can't agree more. If you flood them with scary shit from the moment they start reading, they're going to be anesthetised to their fear by the midway point."

When an attractive waitress came to take their order, Tim suggested Jason try their draft NOLA. The two settled into a comfortable conversation about writing, success, what defines horror and where the genre was going.

Two drinks later, Tim suggested food.

They ordered burgers, Cajun fries and a Caesar salad for them to split.

Halfway through the meal, Tim put down his burger, wiped ketchup off his chin and took a long, deep breath. After a moment of contemplation, he gave Jason a big smile and asked, "Have you seen them yet?"

Chapter 3

"Seen who?" Jason asked, confused.

"The shadows," Tim replied.

"I don't understand … what shadows?"

"You've just answered my question; you obviously haven't yet noticed them. That's a good thing. I need you to listen to what I have to say with an open mind – what I am about to tell you is deadly serious. While it's going to sound like a plot from one of my books, or one of yours for that matter, it's not."

Jason could tell from Tim's expression that he was indeed being serious. "Okay. Consider me suitably creeped out. What's the deal with the shadows?"

"There are powers and energies within our world that remain unseen and unknown. Most of them are innocuous. Some, however, are not only dangerous, but have developed sentient capabilities. The most dangerous are the ones we call the long shadows."

Jason gave the other man a doubting look. He was starting to think that his writing idol was setting him up for some sort of mega punk as part of his initiation to the group.

"Before you make up your mind based solely on your own incredulity, please hear me through," Tim requested.

"Does every newcomer get this speech?" Jason asked.

"It depends on who is chosen to alert the new member, but, yes, even if the wording is different, everyone is told about the shadows."

"All writers or just horror writers?"

"Just horror writers."

"Hmmm…" Jason smirked, unconvinced. He sat back and crossed his arms, waiting for Tim to explain himself.

"There comes a point in the life of a horror author when the writing takes on more depth, and in certain cases their fictional accounts begin to parallel an unknown reality. There are dark forces that surround us and have probably existed on this planet since the very beginning. When a writer's words begin to shed light on the possibility of that reality, that writer becomes of great interest to them. It is at that point that horror writers down through the ages have inadvertently written about evil entities that hide in the shadows and seem to be observing our every move."

"Wait a minute," Jason interrupted. "This sounds awfully like the Bodachs in Dean Koontz's book."

"He freely admits that they were his inspiration for the Bodachs, however his creatures were attracted to sudden and violent death. The long shadows are attracted by the writer's mind and imagination. They want to know if their world has in fact been discovered or whether the horror writer is simply spinning his own web of dark manifestations."

"Why would they care?" Jason asked.

"Because they have survived for millions of years and remained invisible to all creatures including humankind. If someone has indeed become aware of their existence, they need to know, so that they can protect themselves."

"Oh come on," Jason said, shaking his head.

"When, in the 18th century, the public first began adopting horror as a legitimate writing genre, some of the creators of the darker gothic tales began sensing that something was observing them," Tim continued, ignoring Jason's interruption. "It wasn't until a writer vanished without a trace that others banded together. It would seem that the missing writer had not been alone at the time and that his friend, another writer, witnessed his disappearance from across the room. For the first time, horror writers began to openly discuss their concerns. When they learned that all of them had sensed, and in some cases, seen the same thing, it became clear that something untoward was afoot. They formed an informal dinner club and began a tradition of inviting new writers whose work was leaning towards the darker recesses of existence, to dine with them. They would then use that opportunity to apprise the new member of all that they knew and what exactly they should do to best ensure their safety."

"This is a gag right? Some sort of hazing for a new member?"

"Not at all. These dinners exist for the sole purpose of warning writers such as yourself, who have wandered into a realm of paranormal darkness that does not want to be discovered."

"But I haven't discovered anything. All the dark creepy stuff comes entirely from my own imagination," Jason insisted.

"But they don't know that. They see you writing about

things that are not as fictional as you think, and may even be encroaching on the truth of their existence."

"What are you suggesting? Jason asked. "That I'm channelling some sort of dark force?"

"Not at all, but from having read some of your work, I know from experience that you will have, by now, attracted their interest."

"What exactly are they?"

"We don't know what they are. We're not even certain that the shadow is a part of their actual being or whether it's just their way of concealing themselves to study us."

"So, are they hiding in the shadows?" Jason asked.

"No. The shadow is almost certainly a part of them. The only time you can ever be certain that you've seen one of them is usually in a bright room with lots of ambient light. When one of them is in the room with you, you will notice a very subtle shadow where one shouldn't exist.

"Let me tell you about the first time I noticed one. I had been warned at the dinner a few years earlier but had never seen even the slightest trace of one in my house. I was working in my office. It was a bright day and the room was almost completely devoid of shadows. I was working on book one of the *Deadish* series and was writing an especially scary chapter when I noticed that our bookcase was casting a long shadow out towards my desk. At first I thought nothing else about it until I remembered what I'd been told at my first dinner. I also remembered the one sacred rule when in any a doubt as to whether they were there."

"What's the rule?" Jason asked as a slight chill ran up his back.

"Never acknowledge that you've seen them."

"How do you do that...or not do that?"

"Don't stare directly at the shadow. The best way is to only use your peripheral vision. That's what I did that day. I first looked around the rest of the room and verified what I already knew, which was that there should not have been any visible shadows other than those directly under the furniture. I then looked out the corner of my eye and verified that there was indeed a light grey shadow angling towards where I was sitting."

"And you felt that it was one of these creatures?" Jason asked.

"Not immediately. It wasn't until I broke for lunch and sat in the kitchen that I was certain."

Why then?"

"Because it followed me in there," Tim explained. "When I walked in, there were no shadows in the brightly lit room, then after making myself a sandwich and sitting at the table, I noticed that the fridge was casting a shadow out into the centre of the room."

"What happens in a darker room where there are a lot of shadows and unlit spaces?"

"Like here?" Tim asked.

"Yes. Exactly like here."

"Keep looking directly at me, but use your peripheral vision."

"When?" Jason asked.

"Now," Tim replied as he turned to the bartender and gave him a brief nod.

The man walked to a series of wall switches and flipped

them all on. The place was suddenly bathed in bright light. Jason was about to question what the hell was going on when, out of the corner of his eye, he saw countless light grey shadows where no shadows should have been cast.

Tim gestured again to the bartender and the man turned the lights back off.

"What the fuck did I just see?" Jason asked in barely a whisper.

"The two of us sitting in a dark bar having a quiet conversation was too tempting for them."

"So they can hear and understand us?"

"We don't think so. You can talk about them as much as you like, just don't write about them."

"These things can read?" Jason asked.

"I don't know if it's reading as we think of it, but they seem able to recognise and possibly even understand the meaning of visible text. We believe that that is how they know when an author is getting close to being aware of their existence."

The conversation was put on pause as their meal was cleared and another round of drinks placed in front of them.

"So what exactly happens if someone does look at them?" Jason asked as he downed half his pint.

"I personally only know of one writer that has done so," Tim replied. "He called me right after he inadvertently looked directly at a shadow. He started to tell me that it was rising up from the floor and reforming into something."

"Reforming into what?"

"I don't know. The call ended. Nobody ever saw or heard from him again. He just disappeared."

"That's impossible," Jason said. "There must have been some evidence left behind in his home."

Tim sighed and leaned across the table. "There was no evidence of a crime. His house was completely empty. It was as if he had never existed. Nobody had heard of him, including members of the dinner club. If you google him, nothing comes up. No books, no wiki ... nothing."

"But you remember him," Jason said.

"I think it had something to do with my having been on the phone with him when it happened, whatever it was."

"I'm confused. If the entities are capable of erasing all trace of someone who has openly noted them, how are the dinner club members aware of them? If all witnesses disappear and nobody has a memory of them, the writers shouldn't know of them either."

"Their ability to erase a person from existence has one flaw. If they remove someone while another person is either present or, as in my case, tied to them via a phone or video connection, that person somehow keeps the memory of the writer. There haven't been that many witnesses to an erasure, but there have been enough to keep the knowledge alive."

"Why do they leave the witness behind?" Jason asked. "Surely that's the last thing they would do."

"You would think so, but so long as the witness did not themselves acknowledge the entity, they are left alone."

"What sort of creature could have the power to eradicate someone's entire existence?"

"The sort that nobody knows about. The sort that goes out of its way to ensure that its existence is secret."

"Why haven't you told the press or the authorities?"

"Because the first thing that would happen would be that the person we told would write a report or worse, a story. At that point the most likely result would be widespread erasure of anyone connected to the knowledge. Imagine an entire newspaper vanishing without any trace of it ever having existed."

"Do you really think they are that powerful?" Jason asked.

"I think it's best not to find out. As far as we know, horror writers seem to be the only humans that are aware of them and we should keep it that way. We don't have a clue what they are. It's perfectly possible that they could be capable of erasing the entire population."

"To what gain?" Jason asked. "Why do they even care if we know about them?"

"Don't forget that these entities have probably existed on earth since the dawn of time. They have seen mankind evolve into sentient beings that automatically destroy anything they don't understand."

"Why would they think that we were capable of doing them any harm? We can't even look directly at them."

"Let me ask you a question," Tim said. "Let's say you had been observing a species that systematically kills for sport, food or even greed, and then suddenly, one day, it became aware that you had been spying on them. Would you, considering their predisposition to violence, feel safe letting them carry on as before? Or would you decide that the safest course of action would be to eradicate the species altogether?"

"I think you know my answer."

Tim shrugged. "Hence the need for our small group to do what we can to ensure that the shadows continue to feel unthreatened by the human race."

"That's one hell of a responsibility," Jason commented.

"Nobody ever said writing horror was easy," Tim said, smiling.

The two men stayed in the bar for another hour. Tim stuck to beer but Jason, his nerves pretty much shot, turned to the New Orleans staple, Sazerac, a blend of rye whiskey, bitters and absinthe. By the time the two returned to the hotel, Jason was having trouble walking and focussing his eyes while Tim seemed relatively sober.

The doorman was so used to guests drunkenly stumbling in that Jason's condition hardly even registered with him. Tim walked him to his room and made sure Jason made it to the bed in one piece.

Jason passed out cold. It wasn't until he began having repetitive dreams about drinking water that he finally came around if only to stagger to the mini bar and down two bottles of San Pellegrino. For a split second he felt better, then his stomach rebelled against the earlier alcohol and the current influx of fizzy liquid.

Jason only just managed to make it to the bathroom before projectile vomiting his dinner, five pints of beer and a good quantity of highly acidic Sazerac. Thankfully his sudden expulsion of stomach contents was successfully aimed into the vintage style toilet, despite the room being in complete darkness.

Jason stood back up on shaky legs and turned on the

bathroom lights. The room was suddenly bathed in bright, white illumination that caused him to flinch and squint as he approached the basin.

He stared at his reflection and was shocked at the face that looked back at him. His skin had a yellowish tinge to it and his eyes seemed to be resting on a pair of puffy bags he didn't remember ever seeing before. As if that wasn't bad enough, his skin was glistening with oily sweat as his body desperately tried to leech out the poison.

Jason splashed some cold water on his face and dried himself with a ludicrously small hand towel. He took one last look at himself and was about to turn away when something caught his eye.

The bright overhead lights produced no shadowing within the room, and yet, a decorative, antique cabinet against the far wall had a long, light grey shadow stretching out in front of it.

Jason remembered clearly what Tim Hall had told him, however, in his unsteady and possibly still inebriated state, he found himself feeling defiant. After all, it was just a shadow.

Jason sat on the side of the bath and stared down at the grey shape. It didn't appear dangerous in any way. It just lay there. As he was about to head back to bed, the shadow moved. It was hardly perceptible at first, but then it started to elongate as if stretching closer to Jason.

He watched, fascinated as the tip of the elongation reached his foot.

"What are you up to, little guy?" Jason slurred.

The shadow detached from the cabinet and started to

swirl around his feet. After a few moments it began to lift off the floor, looking almost like a tiny patch of dense fog. Soon it reached Jason's ankles.

For a moment, he felt a gentle warming.

Then he felt nothing but pain.

Chapter 4

Tim Hall woke up in his hotel room feeling the effects of too much beer. He switched on his bedside light and reached for some water. A piece of hotel stationary sat folded, leaning against his glass. Tim often had thoughts or ideas in the middle of the night and wrote himself a note so as not to forget the next day.

He opened it and found it to be blank, or at least that was his first impression. Knowing full well that he wouldn't have left an empty note to himself, he turned on the side light and examined it more carefully.

There was no writing to be seen, however, maybe because of his love of detective novels, he thought to angle the paper a few different ways and saw that indentations were just visible on the white surface. Tim went to his MacBook case and retrieved a Number 2 pencil. He held the lead almost flat against the paper and very gently began to rub. After a few seconds, he was able to discern that there was writing. The indented area stood out as white lettering on the page. He immediately recognised the writing. It was his.

It read:

Remember to check in with him in morning. Not sure if fully understood everything. Perhaps another talk?

Tim looked at the note for a long time before shaking his head and crumpling it into a ball. He often wrote down notes in the middle of the night as a reminder. Some were useful, but that one didn't jog his memory at all. Obviously he needed to talk to someone about something, but that could relate to just about anything and anyone. He decided not to worry about it. If it was that important, it would make sense at some point.

Tim rubbed his eyes and started thinking about that night's upcoming dinner. He always looked forward to the Dark Hearts event even though for the last four years there had been no new member to induct into the group.

In one way it was a relief. It meant that the new horror writers weren't getting too close to the wrong side of their creative darkness.

The side that brought them under the scrutiny of the dark shadows.

LASTING MEMORIES

Chapter 1

Liam Grant didn't want any new friends. The ones he had were bad enough. The whole pack were a bunch of selfish, narcissistic phonies. Even the people from his past job that he'd thought were friends had all tuned their backs on him the moment he was let go.

Liam was happier alone anyway. He would have preferred to have been able to keep his little condo by the marina, but without an income, the monthly mortgage payments had taken care of whatever savings he might have had. What really sucked was that he'd managed to keep the condo rented while he was in Jail, but those funds soon found their way into the pocket of his attorney leaving him with nada.

He'd at least hoped that by selling the unit, he'd have had some money left over, but apparently, he was what they called 'underwater' in his mortgage. The aquatic term meant that his home wasn't even worth the loan amount, let alone being able to provide him with some funds from the equity he thought he had in it.

After the foreclosure sale, the bank told Liam that he still owed them money. When he told them that he didn't have any, they told him they were going to garnish his wages. After reminding them that he had no job from which to take any wages from, they stopped talking to him altogether.

The last straw was when Liam ended up selling his fifteen-year-old Honda just so he could pay for a month-and-a-half's rent at the Grand Manor apartments on Western Avenue, a few blocks north of Wilshire. The apartment came furnished, which was a good thing considering that the bank had sold what little he'd had at auction. It was a one bedroom with a kitchenette and a bathroom that looked to have all its original fittings from when it was built in the early 1930s.

The unit was on the sixth floor which usually meant that there would be some sort of view. Not in number 626. The living room and bedroom were home to the only two windows in the apartment, and both looked across an alleyway to a dilapidated brick building that gave no clue as to its function. The place had no windows above the first floor. Faded lettering that said 'BE KIND' was barely legible despite having been painted in ten-foot-high letters.

Liam would have asked the front desk what those words had to do with the building, but there was no front desk. Despite there being over a hundred units in the Grand Manor, there was no onsite manager or handyman.

On a message board next to the rarely functioning elevator, a laminated notice said simply, 'FOR HELP CALL 323 634 5500'.

Liam had called once when he first moved in and found he had no hot water. He never once spoke to a human. He was instructed to leave a message by a robotic phone-tree voice, which he did, then, not surprisingly, never heard another word. Whether by paranormal intervention or what, one week later his taps began to produce a trickle of luke-warm water.

Though Liam often, too often in fact, heard other occupants within the building, he rarely saw anyone. To be fair, much of that was of his own doing. He made a concerted effort whenever he was in any of the public spaces within the Manor to scuttle away as fast as possible to avoid having to engage in any form of conversation or social interaction.

He'd managed to dodge any encounter with his fellow residents until his second week in the building.

That's when, ten days before Christmas, he'd met Grace.

Liam had just returned to the Grand Manor after an excruciating bus ride from West Hollywood where he'd interviewed to work at a seafood restaurant on Santa Monica Blvd. Liam was neither a foodie nor culinarily skilled, but according to the posting, none of those attributes were required. They were looking for part time help scaling and gutting fish, washing dishes and cleaning up after closing.

The owner had taken one look at Liam and suggested that, just maybe, he wasn't the best fit for the restaurant. Liam was about to argue the point when the woman led him backstage into the kitchen. Even though it was hours before opening, the place was a hive of activity, and the smell of fresh fish was almost overpowering. Every single kitchen employee was young enough to be his offspring. All were heavily inked and studded and seemed to work as one autonomous collective as they prepped for the lunch rush.

Through some sort of kitchen telepathy, the staff

seemed to sense his being there and all turned towards him at the same time. Their hard stares and heavily inked faces took him back to a buried memory from the time he'd spent at the California State Prison in Corcoran.

Liam left the restaurant without saying another word.

Back at the Manor, Liam had just stepped into the elevator and was about to press his floor button, when a weak voice asked him to hold the door for her.

The woman must have come into the building only second after him, but Liam hadn't even noticed her. He desperately wanted to let the door slide shut leaving him alone in the confined space, but there was something about the woman that made him, for once, offer a modicum of kindness.

He lay his arm against the elevator door and despite its continued attempts to close, Liam held fast until she had joined him.

The moment the door rumbled shut, Liam could smell an almost overpowering waft of rose petals and moth balls. While not a particularly pleasant aroma, it reminded him of his late grandmother. When Liam was a young boy, almost half a century earlier, his mother used to take him to visit his grandma in her tiny condo in Santa Monica. He hadn't thought of her or her tidy little home in years, but the rose water and mothball bouquet took him right back there.

"Thank you," the woman said as she turned to face the closed elevator door.

"Which floor do you want?" Liam asked.

"Same as you please. Lucky number six."

Liam was uncomfortable with her knowing which floor

he lived on, but he supposed that, just because he didn't care who lived in the building, others still did and paid attention.

As the elevator creaked its way up to the sixth floor, Liam wondered what the woman did when it wasn't running, which was most of the time. He'd gotten used to the stairs, but from the brief glance he'd had at her beseeching face when she asked him to hold the door, he noted that she looked ancient. Liam wasn't exactly a spring chicken himself, but she had to have at least another forty or so years on him.

With a worrying shudder, the elevator stopped, and the door opened with slow, poorly maintained reluctance. Liam gave it a little boost with his arm then held it open so the woman could exit.

As Liam stepped out behind her, he realised that he had a problem. She was heading off to the right in the same direction that he needed to go, and she was slow. Very, very slow. She also seemed to weave a little, resulting in her taking up most of the width of the dimly lit hallway. There was no way he could pass her yet he felt extremely uncomfortable shuffling along behind her. Besides, if he did pass her, she would end up seeing which unit was his and that was completely unacceptable.

"You should go ahead of me," she said, flattening herself against the wall. "It'll take me much longer than you to get to my door. I'm at the far end."

"It's no problem," Liam said. "You take your time."

"That's nice of you but unnecessary. 626 is only halfway along the hallway. You don't need to wait on me."

Crap, Liam thought to himself. She already seemed to know where he lived.

Liam gave her as warm a smile as he could muster then stepped by her. He made a conscious effort not to touch her despite the narrowness of the hallway, but as he passed, he again smelled the roses and camphor only this time, because of their proximity, his nose picked up something else. It was sweet yet at the same time a little sickly. It was intermingled with the other scents and seemed to get caught at the back of his throat.

Liam had his keys out before he even reached his door. He knew he should say something to the woman just to be polite, but as was his way, he chose instead to step wordlessly into his shabby unit and double bolt the door behind him. He stood there for a good few minutes trying to recover from having had to engage with another human being.

Liam hadn't always been like that. In fact, before the accident, back when he'd thought that driving after an evening of drinking and doing a little blow did nothing to diminish his driving skills or reflexes, he'd been extremely social. Maybe even too social if that was possible. But ever since the moment his Range Rover obliterated the other car, Liam had changed. He still, at least once a day, replayed the crash in his head, each time wondering if there was something else he could have done to avoid the impact.

The woman who'd been driving must not have seen Liam or his SUV because she started a U-turn right smack dab in front of him. Even though the accident was her fault, he was found to be legally intoxicated and therefore responsible for the deaths.

After months in hospital, then years in courtrooms for

the two counts of second-degree murder, plus the resulting six years in prison, the experience had turned him from a party animal into a wretch that was scared of his own shadow.

On the rare occasion when he permitted himself the luxury of reflection, he still couldn't believe that he'd gone from being a hot shot executive at Global Studios, to living in a shit hole like the Grand Manor without even enough money to continue living there for very much longer.

He was about to collapse onto the tired and mildly aromatic sofa when the battery-operated doorbell chimed, rattling itself against the stained stucco wall.

"Mister Grant," the frail voice said from the other side of the door. "It's Grace Milford. We just met in the elevator. I wonder if I could bother you for a second."

Liam sighed deeply as he reached for the deadbolt and chain.

Chapter 2

"I know that this is a lot to ask, but would you mind seeing if you could fix my toilet? It doesn't seem to want to stop flushing."

"I'm not a plumber," Liam replied, bluntly.

"I know you're not, but I've left messages with the management company, and they're not getting back to me. I'm on a fixed budget and hearing that water just running away is terrifying. I don't know if I'll be able to pay the bill."

Liam was about to say no when he saw that her eyes had teared over. "Let me have a look," he replied as he sensed his comfort zone drift away on a wave of rose petals and camphor.

Liam double locked his door despite only going less than a hundred feet down the hallway.

"If you're going to visit my home, I should probably introduce myself," she said with a fragile smile.

"I think you already did, when you rang my doorbell."

"Did I? Yes, I suppose I did."

"How long have you lived here?" Liam asked, feeling he should say something.

"Since long before these apartments were rental units. My husband bought the place just after the war."

"Vietnam?" Liam asked, taking a stab in the dark.

Grace laughed. "Oh dear, no. World War II," she corrected him. "We moved in here in 1948."

"Wow, I've never stayed longer than a couple of years in any one place." Liam replied, omitting the six years he spent in an 8 by 6 prison cell.

"That's a pity," Grace said as they finally reached her front door. "The stability of a home is an important thing."

"I wish I'd known that a little sooner." Liam shrugged.

Grace reached out and turned the old brass door handle to unit 658. The door swung open on squeaky hinges as she stood aside to let him pass. Liam was a little surprised that the elderly woman hadn't bothered to lock her door.

"Do you always leave your place unlocked?" he asked.

"Since the day we moved in," she replied.

Liam slid past her and stepped into her modest entry hall.

"William and I always believed that if you adopt the reality that you might be burgled, you probably will be. I've always refused to accept such a likelihood and have never once had a break in."

"Sort of like mind over matter?" Liam suggested.

"Something like that," Grace replied as she reached for the light switch.

With more illumination, Liam could immediately see that the apartment was much bigger than his. There was a full-sized kitchen, a substantial living room and a hallway with four other doors leading off it.

"How does that work, with you owning a unit in a rental building?" Liam asked.

"Very nicely, actually. When this neighbourhood began

its decline in the late sixties, ownership of the apartments began to fall. By the next decade there were only twenty or so full-time residents. When the condo association voted to sell the entire property, I was terrified of losing my home."

"I'm surprised it wasn't bought by a developer who intended to knock it down and build something else."

"Oh, they couldn't do that. Though you might not be able to see it now, this was a famous landmark back in its day and was named an historic property by the city of Los Angeles. It can never be torn down, though considering the neglect of the management company, it wouldn't surprise me if it fell down on its own. Besides, I knew the new owner very well, and was given special dispensation to stay in my apartment."

"That's good to hear," Liam said. "So, where's this running toilet?"

"This way." Grace led him to her bedroom and for a brief second, Liam remembered the scene in the movie *Yes Man* when Jim Carrey is seduced by an elderly woman in a surprisingly similar circumstance.

"The toilet's in there," Grace pointed to a closed door.

Sure enough, the moment he opened it, he could hear running water. He peered under the avocado-coloured toilet-seat lid and saw water streaming into the bowl. Liam removed the top of the cistern and looked inside. The problem was obvious. The flap that was meant to seal the out-flow once the tank had emptied, was broken.

"This is a simple fix," Liam announced. "I can pick up a new part tomorrow if you want."

"That would be terribly kind." Grace beamed. "What

about the running water in the meantime?"

"I could shut off the valve, but you wouldn't be able to use the toilet until I fix it."

"There's a powder room just off the entry hall. I can use that one."

"Good." Liam lowered himself down onto what looked to be the original green tiling and reached for the water supply valve. Liam could see that it wasn't that much newer that anything else in the bathroom and prayed that it would work.

It did, and as he turned it to the closed position, the water stopped pouring into the bowl and the room quietened.

"And you told me you weren't a plumber," Grace said as she gave him a tiny round of applause.

"I'll pick up the part in the morning and swing by to install it. Will you be around in the morning?"

"I usually am," she replied with a hint of sadness in her voice. "Let me give you some money. How much do you think the part will cost?"

Liam was as near broke as he'd ever been in his life and momentarily considered overcharging the old woman before ridding himself of the notion. "If I go to Home Depot in Hollywood, it'll probably be five dollars or less," he answered honestly.

"You must let me pay you for your trouble," Grace insisted.

"It's no trouble. Let's just call it a neighbourly act," Liam said, surprising himself at his newfound and unwarranted generosity.

"Well, you must let me thank you in some way."

Liam was concerned that their dialogue was getting awfully close to that of the Jim Carrey movie. If her next line involved him getting comfortable so she could help him relax, he was going to hightail to it out of there and never look back.

"I know," Grace announced. "You can come over here on Christmas Eve and join me in a glass of sherry and fresh baked mince pies."

"I think I have other plans," Liam said automatically as he always did to any social invite, not that he got many of those anymore.

"Hogwash," she replied. "I can tell another loner from a hundred yards, and you have solitude written all over you."

"I just don't feel comfortable being around other people at the..."

"Let's discuss this tomorrow when you install the new part," Grace said as she led him back to her front door.

Once she'd closed it behind him, he stood in the seedy hallway and wondered how he'd gotten himself into such a stupid situation. Then it hit him. He'd agreed to help someone. His mom always used to use the expression 'no good deed goes unpunished' and at that moment, her adage couldn't have been more fitting.

After a miserable interview at the fish place, all he'd wanted to do was sit in his dreary one-bedroom apartment and wallow in the self-pity that had become his one, true companion. Instead, the old lady had given him ten seconds of misty-eyed pleading and he'd rolled over in nothing flat. Well, he got what he deserved. His morning was going be taken up finding the damn part and then installing it. Plus, he now had to find a way of gracefully declining her Christmas Eve invite without hurting her feelings.

The fact that she'd invited him to come by on Christmas Eve only made things exponentially worse. It was on another Christmas Eve, after a studio-wide blow-out party, that he'd ploughed into the Toyota Corolla outside Dale's bookstore on 3rd Avenue.

If there was one day in the year when he didn't want to see or talk to anybody, it was Christmas Eve.

It had been a long time since he'd been included in any seasonal festivities. Once folks found out that he was the Christmas Sleigher (the pun had helped give his case the extra punch it needed to attract the media) he was ostracised by just about everyone.

"Christmas Sleigher," he mumbled to himself as he shook his head miserably at the memory. "Very funny."

Chapter 3

Home Depot didn't have the part. They had a million other frigging parts, but not the one he needed. He was going to tell her to order the thing online but assumed that she was unlikely to do much internet shopping or have a computer at all. His dark side was whispering for him to tell the old biddy that she was SOL. She would just have to use the powder room until someone eventually got back to her from the management company.

Unfortunately, Liam's good side won out as it usually did. He walked up to Los Feliz Blvd and caught the bus to Glendale where he found the part at Lowe's for less that he'd estimated.

It was almost midday by the time he knocked on Grace's door. It took so long for her to answer that he thought for a moment that she'd gone out.

"Liam!" she said, sounding sincerely happy to see him. "Did you find it?"

"Sure did," he replied, leaving out the extra ninety minutes it had taken plus the two bus rides that hadn't been part of his original morning plan.

"Give me two minutes to tidy up back there, then you can do whatever it is that needs doing. Why don't you sit in the living room? There are some magazines and even a TV if you can find anything to watch."

"I'll be fine just sitting," Liam replied as she led him into the spacious room.

Unlike his claustrophobic apartment, her living room had two full-sized windows which looked across Western and down onto Korea Town. Both were spotlessly clean and had a view of Silverlake in the distance.

As Grace shuffled off to tidy up, Liam took in his surroundings. Through the cheerful veneer of Christmas decorations, including a stunningly decorated tree, he could see that the furniture was old but looked expensive and well cared for. Silver frames were dotted around the room, filled with images capturing a split second in time and were now all that was left of a lifetime of memories.

There were some interesting paintings dotted around, but Liam didn't know if the stuff was any good or not. What he did find strange was that on top the mantel piece was a row of urns. Each one was different in size and style, but there was no mistaking the fact they were the type that was usually filled with the remains of a cremated loved one.

Liam approached the fireplace and studied them. On each was a single name. At first, Liam had thought they might be relatives, but some of the names didn't quite fit that supposition. Sure, there was a Mindy and a Clarence which would have worked, but there was also a Tinkerbell, Shadow and a Felix among the group.

"Ah," Grace said as she walked into the room, "you've met my friends."

"I take it these weren't people?" Liam asked.

"Heavens no," Grace giggled. "That would be a little too

morbid to keep that many on the mantlepiece, wouldn't it?"

Liam shrugged.

"These are all my cats."

"No humans at all?" Liam asked. "Not even your husband?"

"I wish William were there among them, but he died in that plane that crashed in the Santa Monica Bay back in the 80s. They never recovered his body, so there was nothing to cremate."

"I'm sorry," Liam mumbled.

"So am I, but one has to just keep on, keeping on, as they say."

Liam wasn't sure how to respond.

Thankfully, Grace added, "the bathroom's free if you're ready."

It only took him a few minutes to remove the old rubber flapper and install the new one. He turned the water back on and watched as it began pouring into the dry tank. Once the float rose to its highest position, the flow stopped the backflow, and the room quietened.

"Grace," Liam called out, "it's fixed."

She appeared a few moments later with a look of complete surprise.

"That was very quick," she commented.

"It was a very simple fix."

"Only to you," she gushed.

"Don't be putting me on too high a pedestal," Liam replied. "The float and the flapper are just about the only things I know how to fix in a toilet."

"The float and the flapper," Grace wistfully repeated.

"Sounds like a risqué novel from the fifties."

Liam burst out laughing. It was rare for him to do so, and it felt weird, almost wrong. He busied himself by collecting the few tools he'd needed for the job as Grace smiled.

"There's nothing wrong with laughter," she opined. "It's good for the body and the soul."

All Liam could do was nod. He knew she was right, but something about her saying the words had struck an emotional nerve. The last thing he wanted was for the elderly woman to see that his eyes had welled up over something so insignificant.

"I know you won't take money for your time, but I insist on paying for the flapper thingy. How much was it?"

"Four seventy-five," Liam replied. "But you really don't have to…"

"Of course I do. I'm glad that you don't charge for kindness, but parts … that's something else entirely."

Grace produced a small change purse from somewhere within the folds of her skirt and carefully counted out the exact amount before handing it to him.

As she led him to the front door, she said, "Don't forget next Saturday."

Liam gave her a questioning look.

"That's Christmas Eve," she reminded him. "You should come by at eleven then we'll both have something to drink and eat before midnight."

Liam was about to take another stab at declining the invite when Grace seemed to read his mind.

"Don't even try to tell me that you have other plans. You

don't, and unless I'm completely mistaken, you haven't had any plans at Christmas for an awfully long time."

Grace was right. Liam couldn't even remember when he'd last shared the holiday with another person, unless you call sitting alone in a Chinese restaurant on Christmas day sharing.

"Why is midnight so important?"

"Because it's the most magical time of the year. It's the moment between a year's worth of anticipation and the actual dawning of Christmas day."

"If I do stop by-" he began.

"Which you will," Grace stated.

"If I do stop by, I doubt I'll be able to stay long. I haven't been up that late in..." Liam had a flash back of his arrest and the night he'd spent in the Santa Monica jail right after the accident. "...a very long time."

"You may leave whenever you wish, though, I think you'll find that you may just not want to."

Liam was amused that she felt that her mince pies and sherry would be sufficient cause for him to hang around for any longer that he really had to.

"What can I bring?" Liam asked, resigning himself to the inevitable.

"Do you have any tuna?" Grace enquired.

"I don't know. Probably. If not, I can pick up a can."

"Excellent," she smiled. "If I don't run into you before, I look forward to seeing you a week from Saturday.

As Liam walked back to his apartment, he couldn't help wondering what he'd let himself in for. It was bad enough spending Christmas by himself, but at least he was used to that. Having to sit with an old lady while she served tuna, mince pies and sherry, and probably babbled on about the good old days before jets and television, sounded like a recipe for a very depressing night.

Once back in his apartment, Liam was about to stretch out on the couch for a quick nap when he had a thought. He walked over to the kitchenette and opened the only above-counter cupboard.

In it was a box of cereal, some cans of chili from the Dollar Store, instant coffee and tucked away at the very back of the thinly populated shelf was a single can of Ralph's generic tuna chunks in spring water. Liam stared at it for a few moments, shuddered, then headed for the couch.

Chapter 4

Liam spent the following week chasing up job openings. The pickings were slim for someone with his criminal record and age, but being that close to Christmas made the postings even harder to find.

The thing that he found the most frustrating was that if it weren't for the damn internet, he could probably find a job and keep it. The problem was, even if an employer didn't do a search on him before hiring him, at some point, they all get curious about their employees and google them. In Liam's case, such a search always led to the boss needing to have a 'serious' conversation prior to 'reluctantly' letting him go.

As he walked back from the bus stop after spending three hours getting to Pacoima and back where he'd been scheduled to interview for a janitorial job at Whiteman Airport, he was as disheartened as he'd ever been.

When he'd arrived at the airport administration office, he'd been kept waiting for over an hour before being told that they'd hired someone earlier in the day. Whether that was true or not, Liam would never know, though by the way the receptionist had been staring at him, he was fairly sure that they'd found out that the Christmas Sleigher himself was the guy who'd applied to mop up the aircraft hangers.

As he passed the local diner that always seemed to have

a line outside it, Liam got a waft of fried bacon and griddled beef. His stomach did a back flip as he fantasised about chomping down on a bacon cheeseburger with curly fries. Sadly, considering his current situation, there was about as much chance of him being able to pay for lunch at a restaurant as there was of him being offered his old job back at Global Studios.

Such was Liam's aroma-induced state of euphoria that he bumped right into Grace without seeing her as she tried to get her key into the Grand Manor front door.

"I'm so sorry," Liam exclaimed as his brain came back into focus. "I guess I was daydreaming."

"No harm done," she replied, her voice sounding a little raspier than usual. "I just hope your head was somewhere dreamy and fun."

Liam helped with the key, then opened the door for her. As she slid past him, he picked up the usual whiff of roses and camphor, but the other scent was still lurking in the background. In fact, if anything, it was a little stronger. He had no idea what the sickly sweet odour could possibly be, and yet, it concerned him.

"Are you okay?" Liam asked as they wedged themselves into the elevator.

"I'm ninety-seven, Liam," she replied, "nothing is okay. Between the aches, the pains and the plumbing in general, it's amazing they haven't taken me out behind the woodshed and finished me off."

"Probably because of the lack of woodsheds in downtown Los Angeles," he joked, trying to add a little levity to counter her remark.

It seemed to work. Grace laughed, but within moments the laughter turned into a coughing fit. It was over almost before it started, but it seemed to drain what little colour she'd had in her face.

"You'll have to excuse me," she said, trying to catch her breath. "Every year around this time, I get one of those nasty little winter colds."

"Do you want to cancel Saturday?" Liam asked, not sure of how he'd feel if she did.

"Absolutely not. I'll be over this by tomorrow. By Saturday, I'll be ready to party my little heart out."

Liam wasn't so sure that she would be ready to party at all. She looked frailer than usual, and as he accompanied her to the end of the hallway, she seemed less steady on feet.

Liam helped her into her apartment and onto her favourite floral armchair, facing the fireplace.

"I'll be fine," Grace said with a half-hearted wave of her hand. "You get on with what it is that you would normally be doing and leave me to have a little doze."

"You're sure you'll be alright?" he asked.

"I've lasted this long, haven't I?" she volleyed back.

As Liam walked to her front door, he glanced back and saw that she'd already fallen asleep. She looked so small nestled in the overstuffed armchair.

Small and very, very, old.

Saturday was no different to any other day. Liam got up late, had a bowl of generic flakes, an instant coffee and a quick shower. Normally, his next activity would have been to go online and check out the job sites, however, it being

Christmas Eve, there was little chance of there being any new listings. Even if there were, who would respond until after the New Year?

Being both a Saturday and a major holiday, the streets of downtown Los Angeles were nearly deserted. The area wasn't graced with any big box or department stores, therefore those who had left their Christmas shopping to the last possible moment had most likely migrated to Glendale, West Hollywood or The Grove.

The one advantage of being a loner, especially considering how broke he was, was that he had nobody to buy presents for.

Suddenly, the image of Grace, opening her door to him later that night and him having no more than a can of cheap tuna to give to her, seemed to be, even for him, socially unacceptable.

Liam decided to make his way up to Larchmont Village and see if there was some little trinket he could find for next to nothing. The walk took just over fifteen minutes, and Liam regretted the time and effort the moment he reached Larchmont Blvd.

The place was a zoo.

Traffic was backed up in every direction and red-faced drivers were all hunting for any sign of a car pulling back from the diagonal, on-street parking spaces. One look at their darting eyes and twitching faces showed the intensity of their quest. It was almost primordial.

Horns were blaring, voices were raised, and the sidewalks were jammed with shoppers. Liam took a moment to study the expressions of the people as they looked frantically in each and every display window, hungry for inspiration on what to buy next.

Liam wanted nothing to do with the crowds or the anxiety-ridden vibe that he could both see as well as sense. Just as he was about to turn away from the melee, he noticed a beauty supply store that seemed to be of little interest to the other shoppers.

By the time Liam had crossed the street and fought his way through the torrent of humanity, he knew what to buy Grace. On the day he'd first met her, she'd been wearing a simple, faded and well-worn pink bow in her hair.

How much could a bow cost?

The store staff were young and hip, instantly making him feel sorely out of place. Apart from the depressingly large generational gap between him and the salespeople, Liam felt a wave of nerves and embarrassment at having to ask for something so trivial as a hair bow. He was contemplating leaving the store when a young Asian man approached him.

"Can I help you?" he asked.

"Do you have hair ribbons or bows?" Liam managed to ask.

"Absolutely. They're totally coming back into fashion," he advised while briefly checking out Liam's wardrobe which would never be back in fashion, if indeed it ever was.

Liam was shown to a display carousel that must have had hundreds of different ribbons and bows hanging lengthwise from suspended metal hooks.

"Did you have an idea of colour or pattern?" the man asked.

"Wow," Liam said, staring at the vast selection. "Maybe something Christmassy?"

The man studied the display then reached out and removed a bow that had horizontal stripes of green, red and gold.

"This is about as Christmassy as you're going to get."

"I like it," Liam said, with surprising sincerity.

The man turned it over. "You're in luck, it's on sale."

Chapter 5

Liam rang Grace's doorbell at eleven o'clock sharp. In the moment before she opened the door, Liam wondered if she was going to look as frail as she had the other day. He needn't have worried. Standing in her entry hall, dressed in what must have once been an expensive red evening gown, she looked the very picture of health. Her complexion looked normal, and her blue eyes seemed to be particularly clear and sparkling.

Liam felt drastically underdressed. He was wearing jeans and a dark green crew neck under a tan coloured jacket. He was about to apologise for looking so shabby when Grace took his hand and gently pulled him into her home.

"You look amazing," Liam said.

"So do you," she replied. "Go get settled in the living room while I pour you a drink. Sherry all right?"

Grace must have picked up his momentary hesitation.

"I have other options," she said.

"The truth is, I've never had a sherry in my life. I have no idea if I'll like it."

"What's your usual tipple?" Grace asked, amused.

"I used to be a bourbon man."

"Used to be?"

"When I was younger," Liam added. "I don't drink much anymore."

"Is that because of the accident?"

Liam felt as if he'd been punched in the gut.

"There's no need for you to be upset," Grace said as she led him to the living room. "I checked you out online. I know I must seem beyond decrepit, but you'd be surprised how much time I spend on the internet. I looked you up, just to make sure you weren't some serial killer. I also looked up the cost of that flapper thingy."

"Why?" Liam asked.

"Why did I look you up or the price?" she replied.

"Both, I guess."

"I very rarely have anyone in my home anymore and need to feel safe on the rare occasion when I do. As for the price of the flapper ... I wanted to see if you were being fair to me. You'd be surprised how often people try to swindle the elderly out of every last cent they can."

"How'd I do?" Liam asked.

"Well, you're certainly not a serial killer, though you have had a difficult life over the past eight years. As for fixing my toilet, if the figures on Yelp were accurate, you could have charged me $50 and I still would have gotten a good deal. You only charged me $4.75. Why?

"Because I didn't think it was fair to charge you more that the part actually cost. Pardon my assumption, but with you living in the Grand Manor apartments just like me, money must be tight for you as well. I had nothing better to do, so I couldn't see myself charging you for time which is the one thing I have plenty of."

"Even though money has to be a concern for you?"

Liam simply shrugged his shoulders.

"You sit down while I get you a bourbon," Grace advised.

"Actually, I think my bourbon days may be behind me. I'll try that sherry if you don't mind."

Liam had seen images of people drinking sherry out of pretentious little glasses and was worried that if he kept asking for a refill, he'd come across as being a little too attached to the demon drink.

His concern was unwarranted as Grace reappeared with two tumblers half-filled with amber liquid.

"I hope you don't mind, but I hate those tiny little sherry glasses. I find these to be far more suited to celebratory drinking."

"What are we celebrating?" Liam asked as Grace handed him his glass.

"Christmas, life … everything," Grace said as she raised her drink in a toast. "To long life, to lasting memories, to our hearts being full and to our friends always being close by."

"I'm not sure I've experienced that last part for a while, but … cheers." He lifted his glass then took his first taste of sherry.

"Cream sherry is too sweet, and Amontillado is too dry," Grace announced. "I prefer the Oloroso. That's what we're drinking tonight."

"It's delicious," Liam said as he involuntarily licked his lips.

They drank, ate mince pies and talked for the next fifty minutes. Liam found her to be great company. She did tell stories of what she referred to as the golden days, but they were fascinating, some were even funny.

When Liam noticed Grace checking her watch, he saw that it was getting close to midnight.

"I hope you don't mind," he said as he reached into the pocket of his jacket, "I wanted to give you this little present to say thank you for having me over. It's been a long time since anyone's treated me with any sense of hospitality."

Grace took the small, gift-wrapped box and opened it with all the excitement of a young child at Christmas. When she saw the bow, her free hand shot to her mouth. She was clearly moved.

"I hope it's alright," Liam said. "I saw you wearing one when we first met and thought you'd like one for Christmas."

"Oh, Liam. That is so kind of you. The one I still wear was a gift from my husband one Christmas a few years before he died. Though you wouldn't know it now, it was bright red when he gave it to me. Just like everything else my age, it's faded quite badly."

Grace carefully clipped the bow on the side of her head, nestled among her curly grey hair.

"Now for my surprise," she announced. She stepped into the kitchen and reappeared with Liam's can of tuna, now opened, and placed it in the centre of the coffee table.

She approached the mantelpiece and stood in front of each of the twelve urns, then, almost ceremonially, removed the tops.

Liam was about to ask what she was doing when she returned to her seat and checked her watch again.

"Only a few seconds to go," she announced. "Close your

eyes."

"But I don't-" Liam started to say.

"Close them now," she said with a little more urgency.

Liam closed his eyes and sat in almost complete silence. The only sound came from a grandfather clock situated against the far wall.

The room was suddenly filled with the first chime of midnight. Liam counted the next eleven soundings from the antique timepiece, then silence again descended upon the room.

Liam was about to say something when he heard a noise. He wasn't sure what it was at first. It almost sounded like a gentle, repeating rumble coming from somewhere close in the room. As he listened intently, he heard more of the rumbling sounds. Soon, they were everywhere.

"You can open your eyes now," Grace whispered.

The first thing Liam noticed was that Grace had turned her side light off, so the only illumination within the room was coming from the Christmas tree lights. The second thing he saw were the cats.

Or at least the backlit outline of cats.

"Liam, I'd like to introduce you to my friends. First there's Hilda, she was with me when I was still in school." Grace patted her lap and one of the feline outlines jumped up and curled upon her red dress. As Liam looked on, he saw that the animal was gaining definition. He could tell that Hilda was in fact a ginger tabby with one white ear and one black one.

Grace introduced Liam to all twelve of her friends. By the end of the introduction, all of them were curled or draped across her. Their purring filled the room and gave Liam a feeling of peace and tranquillity.

Over the next hour, each animal, now fully back to how they'd looked in life, found their way onto Liam's lap. At one point, three of them were curled upon him, all purring contentedly. Liam felt his eyes start to close as sleep began to pull him down into a blissful oblivion.

Liam had no idea what time it was when he woke. He looked at his watch and saw that it was almost four in the morning. He looked over at Grace and saw that the cats were gone. She was sleeping with her head cocked to one side. She was smiling with her eyes closed and her Christmas ribbon still in place, giving her the appearance of a much younger woman.

Liam smiled too until he noticed the way her arm was hanging limp by the side of her favourite chair.

"No," he cried. "God, no!"

Chapter 6

Liam stayed in Grace's apartment until her body had been removed and he'd given all his details to the attending officer. He returned to his apartment and did the one thing he hadn't done since the accident eight years earlier.

He cried.

Other than going out to stock up on milk and cereal, Liam stayed in his apartment for days. He felt adrift. For some reason, that silly old woman had rekindled enough of his emotions for her death to be almost unbearable. It wasn't as if they'd known each that long or were even that close, yet her passing felt as if yet another door had slammed shut in his miserable life.

As the days passed and he started thinking about his situation; he knew he had to continue looking for work. The problem was that he didn't feel like facing the outside world. All the crowds and commotion could wait a little longer.

Liam was about to take his first shower in days when his doorbell rattled and chimed. The only person who'd ever come to his apartment had been Grace, and she was certainly in no condition to do that anymore.

He opened his door with the security chain still attached and peered out.

"Mr. Hall?" a voice asked.

Liam tried to make out who was standing there but because of the short chain and the door angle, he could only see half a person. The half without the head.

"Mr. Hall, my name is Douglas Feinstein. I am Grace Milford's attorney."

"Don't you mean...you were?" Liam replied.

"Actually, no. I continue to be her lawyer until her estate is fully executed. May I come in?"

Liam was going to say no, but decided that he couldn't really see the harm in hearing the guy out. He was probably just there to invite him to the funeral or something.

"Sure," Liam said as he opened the door. "Sorry for the mess. I like it this way."

Without being asked, Douglas sat at the room's scarred dining table and opened his briefcase. His was older than Liam first thought. His suit looked expensive, and his greying hair was immaculately cut.

Liam remained standing.

"You may want to sit down," Douglas said. "This could take a while."

"How did you find me?" Liam asked.

"Mrs. Milford told me where you lived when we met just before Christmas. If she'd had your phone number, I could have called and arranged for you to stop by my office."

"Why?" Liam asked bluntly.

"To discuss the details of her bequeathment."

Liam laughed before he could stop himself.

"What bequeathment? She lived in the same dump as I do. What could she possibly have had of any value? I mean I've been to her apartment. She has ... had ... some nice old stuff, but I'm not really in the market for a bunch of furniture with nowhere to put it."

It was Douglas' turn to laugh. "Mr. Hall - Grace Milford didn't just live here, she *owned the building*. In addition, she has a living trust that provides an income of, depending on the market, approximately $20,000."

"I guess that was enough for her to live on for a year," Liam said.

"$20,000 a month, Mr. Hall."

"Wow," Liam said, shocked. "So what does that have to do with me?"

"Quite a lot actually. As of last week, you became her primary beneficiary."

Liam stared at the man, thoroughly confused.

"Who was the beneficiary before me?" Liam asked.

"The Canoga Cat Rescue Centre."

"Why did she change it?"

"Don't you worry, they're still getting a nice endowment, but Mrs. Milford decided that she wanted you to have a second chance in life, just as she did."

"I'm not sure I understand."

"Let's just say that before she met and married Mr. Milford, she'd had what some may feel was a checkered past. She'd been arrested for vagrancy and was destined to end up with a custodial sentence. Thankfully, a certain young attorney who was present in the court room on another matter took an interest in her plight and requested that he plead her case. That young man was the late William Milford."

"Still not seeing where I come in," Liam said.

"When you filled out your application to rent a unit within her building, the management company quickly realised who you were and that your circumstances were ... let's say ... a little unusual. They were going to reject your application, but Mrs. Milford overruled them. You weren't aware of it at the time, but she knew that you would be living in the building before you did."

"I don't believe it."

"You should believe it; it's true," Douglas said. "She was quite fascinated by your case and the fact that, by all accounts, she thought you were entirely innocent of the charges. You could have been stone cold sober and not been able to avoid colliding with that car. She felt a certain kinship with you, Mr. Hall. She believed, and as an attorney I have to agree with her, that if you'd had the right representation at the time, you would most certainly not have been found guilty. Just as someone stepped in to change her life for the better, she decided that she wanted to do the same for you. Play it forward, so to speak."

"But we hardly knew each other," Liam insisted.

"She knew you well enough to know that what happened to you was wrong and your life has suffered ever since. I was going to discuss the next part at a later date once you'd come to terms with what I've told you so far, but I may as well tell you the rest while I'm here. In addition to the property and the interest from the trust fund, Mrs. Milford instructed my firm to represent you and have your charges overturned."

"What?"

"You heard me correctly."

"I don't want to go through that again. I mean, that's very nice of her, but even if you could get the case reopened, a retrial would just put my name back in the headlines again. I can just see them: 'The Christmas Sleigher is back.'"

"I have already spoken to the District Attorney's office. This will never go to open court. In fact, if the details of the police investigation and the decisions of the previous DA were to come to light, it would be very embarrassing for the city. While you did collide with Miss Evistone, and both she and her boyfriend died as a result of the crash, none of it was your fault. Miss Evistone had a mix of both benzodiazepine and cocaine in her system. Though this was known to the investigating officer and to the DA's office, it was never revealed in court. Sadly, your lawyer never asked to see the medical records of either casualty during discovery. It would have made all the difference."

"Why did the city cover that up? What did they have against me?"

"Nothing at all. The problem was that the media did a good job destroying your character with their Christmas Sleigher spin. By that point, the city didn't want to be seen helping the defence of someone who had basically already been tried by the court of public opinion."

"So, they let me take the fall just to keep the media-"

"And the public," Douglas added.

"Just to keep them happy?" Liam asked.

"It happens more often than you'd think."

"Are you saying that you actually believe you can get the verdict thrown out?"

"I can guarantee it. It won't be quick, but it will be

private. Nobody wants word of this to get out."

"How long could it take?"

"Probably about eighteen months to two years."

"If you succeed, can I sue them?" Liam asked.

Douglas took a long hard look at the man on the other side of the Formica-topped table.

"The question isn't whether you can, it's whether you should. No matter who was right or wrong, you did cause the death of two people. I'm not sure you want to go to all the trouble of cleaning the slate, only to try and profit from the tragedy. The decision is yours. You can let me know which way you want to go closer to the time."

"No, I can give you an answer now," Liam said. "Grace saw some good in me. I don't want to imagine her looking down and regretting what she's done. Getting the verdict overturned will be enough for me."

"Good," Douglas looked relieved. "That's what she said you'd say."

Liam could only shake his head.

"I need to advise you before we go any further that there is one strict caveat to the bequeathment. In order for you to formally accept the role as her primary beneficiary, you have to sign a letter of agreement to one last codicil within her will."

"Agreement to what?"

"You have to agree to live in her apartment."

"For how long?" Liam asked, stunned.

"Why ... forever, Mr. Hall. Also, you must keep the thirteen urns where they are currently situated on the mantelpiece. In addition, you must be present, within the apartment, every Christmas Eve from eleven at night until at least two o'clock Christmas morning."

"Wait a minute," Liam said. "There are only twelve urns on the mantel piece. I know. I've seen them."

"By next week, there will be one additional urn. It will contain the remains of Mrs. Milford."

Liam was about to say something when all the pennies seemed to drop at the same time.

"If you're in agreement, at least in principle at this point," Douglas said, "we should start going through the preliminary documentation."

Liam nodded as he sat down across from his new attorney.

EPILOGUE

In the twelve months since Grace died, Liam had devoted himself to sprucing up the Grand Manor. He got rid of the old management company and found one that seemed to care about the upkeep of the property and the comfort and safety of the tenants.

Once Grace's apartment formally became his, he had intended to give all her furnishings to charity, but as he started making a list of what to have Goodwill collect, some of the items didn't make the list. He wasn't even sure exactly why, he just knew they had to stay. It was as if he felt that he didn't have the right to dispose of certain belongings that had clearly been important to the previous occupier.

Liam did repaint and have the kitchen and master bathroom modernised, but other than that, he left the apartment the way it was, at least for the time being. Though it was his to do with as he pleased, he felt that a conversation still needed to be had before making any additional modifications.

When Christmas Eve arrived, as per the agreement, Liam was in the apartment at eleven o'clock. Of course, the fact was, he was in the apartment every night. Where else would he be? It was his home. He was watching the movie *Elf* on his new flat screen when his phone alarm went off.

He switched off the TV and walked to the mantlepiece. He carefully removed thirteen lids from their respective urns then turned the room lights off, leaving only the ones on the Christmas tree to provide illumination.

As Liam sat back down in his new recliner, Grace's old grandfather clock started to chime, and Liam closed his eyes. As had happened the previous year, he at first only heard one cat purr. The others soon joined in the chorus until the room was filled with their contented sound and he felt their lithe bodies rubbing against his legs.

He kept his eyes closed wondering what would come next.

He didn't have long to wait.

"Oloroso sherry alright with you?" Grace's familiar voice asked from the kitchen. "Or would you prefer a bourbon?"

THE END